Terry Jones
Fairy Tales

Terry Jones
Fairy Tales

Illustrated by Michael Foreman

SCHOCKEN BOOKS · NEW YORK

First American edition published by Schocken Books 1982
10 9 8 7 6 5 4 3 2 1   82 83 84 85
Published by agreement with Pavilion Books Limited, London

Library of Congress Cataloging in Publication Data

Jones, Terry.
    Fairy tales.
    Summary: A collection of thirty original fairy
tales introducing such beings as the fly-by-night,
the rainbow cat, and the wonderful cake-horse.
    1. Fairy tales—England.   2. Children's stories,
English. [1. Fairy tales.   2. Short stories]
I. Foreman, Michael, 1938–   ill.   II. Title.
PZ8.J555   1982   [Fic]   81-23227
                                    AACR2

Designed by Anthony Cohen
Filmset in Great Britain by BAS Printers Limited, Over Wallop, Hampshire
Printed and bound in Italy by New Interlitho, Milan
ISBN 0-8052-3807-7

These stories were written for Sally Jones
in the summer of 1978

Contents

The Corn Dolly

FARMER WAS CUTTING HIS CORN, when he thought he could hear someone crying far away. Well, he kept on cutting the corn, and the crying got louder and louder until he had only one more shock of corn to cut, and it seemed as if the crying were coming right from it. So he peered into the last bit of corn and sure enough, there was a little creature made of corn stalks, sitting sobbing its heart out.

'What's the matter with you?' asked the farmer.

The little creature looked up and said: 'You don't care,' and went on crying.

The farmer was a kindly man, so he said: 'Tell me what your trouble is, and perhaps there is something I can do.'

'You farmers don't care what happens to us corn dollies,' said the creature.

Now the farmer had never seen a corn dolly before, so he said: 'What makes you think that?'

The corn dolly looked up and said: 'We live in the standing corn, we keep it safe and do no harm to anyone, and yet every year you farmers come with your sharp scythes and cut down the corn and leave us poor corn dollies homeless.'

The farmer replied: 'We have to cut the corn to make the flour to make the bread we eat. And even if we didn't cut it, the corn would wither away in the autumn and you corn dollies would still be homeless.'

But the corn dolly burst into tears again and said: 'Just because we're small and made of straw, you think you can treat us anyhow, and leave us with nowhere to live in the cold winter.'

The farmer said: 'I'll find somewhere for you to live.' And he picked up the corn dolly and took it to the barn and said: 'Look! You can live here and be snug and warm all through the winter.'

But the corn dolly said: 'You live in a fine house made of stone, but just because us corn dollies are small and made of straw, you don't think we're good enough to live in a proper house.'

The farmer said: 'Not at all,' and he picked up the corn dolly and carried it into his house and sat it on the window-sill in the kitchen.

'There,' he said, 'you can live there.'

But the corn dolly scowled and said: 'Just because we're small and made of straw, you think we're not good enough to sit with you and your wife.'

The farmer said: 'Not at all,' and he picked up the corn dolly and carried it to the fireside, and he pulled up a chair and sat the corn dolly down between himself and his wife. But still the corn dolly was not happy.

'What's the matter now?' asked the farmer.

'Just because we're small and made of straw,' said the corn dolly, 'you've sat me on a hard chair, while you and your wife sit in soft chairs.'

'Not at all,' said the farmer, and he gave the corn dolly a soft chair. But still the corn dolly was not happy.

'Is there still something the matter?' asked the farmer.

'Yes,' said the corn dolly. 'Just because I'm small and only made of straw, you've sat me over here, while you and wife sit next to the fire and keep nice and warm.'

The farmer said: 'Not at all. You can sit wherever you like,' and he picked the corn dolly up and put it next to the fire. And just then a spark flew out of the fire and landed on the corn dolly. And, because it was only made of straw, it burst into flames, and, because it was only very small, it was all gone before the farmer or his wife could do anything to save it.

The Silly King

KING HERBERT XII HAD RULED WISELY and well for many years. But eventually he grew very old and, although his subjects continued to love him dearly, they all *had* to admit that as he had grown older he had started to do *very* silly things. One day, for example, King Herbert went out of his palace and walked down the street with a dog tied to each leg. Another time, he took off all his clothes and sat in the fountain in the principal square, singing selections of popular songs and shouting 'Radishes!' at the top of his voice.

Nobody, however, liked to mention how silly their king had become. Even when he hung from the spire of the great cathedral, dressed as a parsnip and throwing Turkish dictionaries at the crowd below, no-one had the heart to complain. In private they would shake their heads and say: 'Poor old Herbert – whatever will he do next?' But in public everyone pretended that the King was as grave and as wise as he had always been.

Now it so happened that King Herbert had a daughter whom, in a moment of slightly more silliness than usual, he had named Princess Fishy – although everyone called her Bonito. Rather conveniently, the Princess had fallen in love with the son of their incredibly rich and powerful neighbour, King Rupert, and one day it was announced that King Rupert intended to pay a state visit to King Herbert to arrange the marriage.

'Oh dear!' said the Prime Minister. 'Whatever shall we do? Last time King Herbert had a visitor, he poured custard over his head and locked himself in the broom cupboard.'

'If only there was someone who could make him act sensibly,' said the Lord Chancellor, 'just while King Rupert's here at any rate.'

So they put up a notice offering a thousand gold pieces to anyone who could help. And from the length and breadth of the land came doctors offering their services, but it was all no use. One eminent doctor had a lotion which he said King Herbert must rub on his head before going to bed, but King Herbert drank it all on the first night, and was very ill. So a second eminent doctor produced a powder to cure the illness caused by the first doctor, but King Herbert put a match to it, whereupon it exploded and blew his eyebrows off. So a third doctor produced a cream to replace missing eyebrows, but King Herbert put it on his teeth and they all turned bright green overnight.

Not one of the doctors could make King Herbert less silly, and he just got ill from their lotions and potions and creams and powders.

Eventually the day of the state visit arrived, and King Herbert was still swinging from the chandeliers in the throne room and hitting people with a haddock.

Everyone was very agitated. The Prime Minister had chewed his nails right down to nothing, and the Lord Chancellor had gnawed through his chain of office, but no-one had any idea of what to do. Just then the Princess Fishy stood up and said: 'Since no-one else can help, let me try.'

'Don't talk nonsense, Bonito!' said the Prime Minister. 'Fifty of the most eminent doctors in the land have failed to cure the King, what could *you* possibly do?'

'I may not be able to cure the King,' said the Princess, 'but if I could show you how to turn an egg into solid gold, then would you do as I said?'

And the Lord Chancellor said: 'Princess, if you could indeed show us how to turn an egg into solid gold, then we should certainly do as you told us.'

'For shame!' said the Princess. 'Then you should do as I say now. I can no more turn an egg into solid gold than you can, but even if I could it wouldn't prove that I could help my father.'

Well, the Lord Chancellor and the Prime Minister looked at each other and, because they had no ideas themselves, and because they had no other offers of help, they agreed to do what the Princess told them.

Shortly afterwards, King Rupert arrived. There were fanfares of trumpets; drums rolled; the people cheered, and they looked for King Rupert's son, but they couldn't see him. King Rupert was dressed in gold and rode a white horse, and on his head he bore the richest crown anyone had ever seen. The Lord Chancellor and the Prime Minister met him at the gates of the town and rode with him down the main street.

Suddenly, just as they were about to enter the palace, an old woman rushed out of the crowd and threw herself in front of King Rupert's horse.

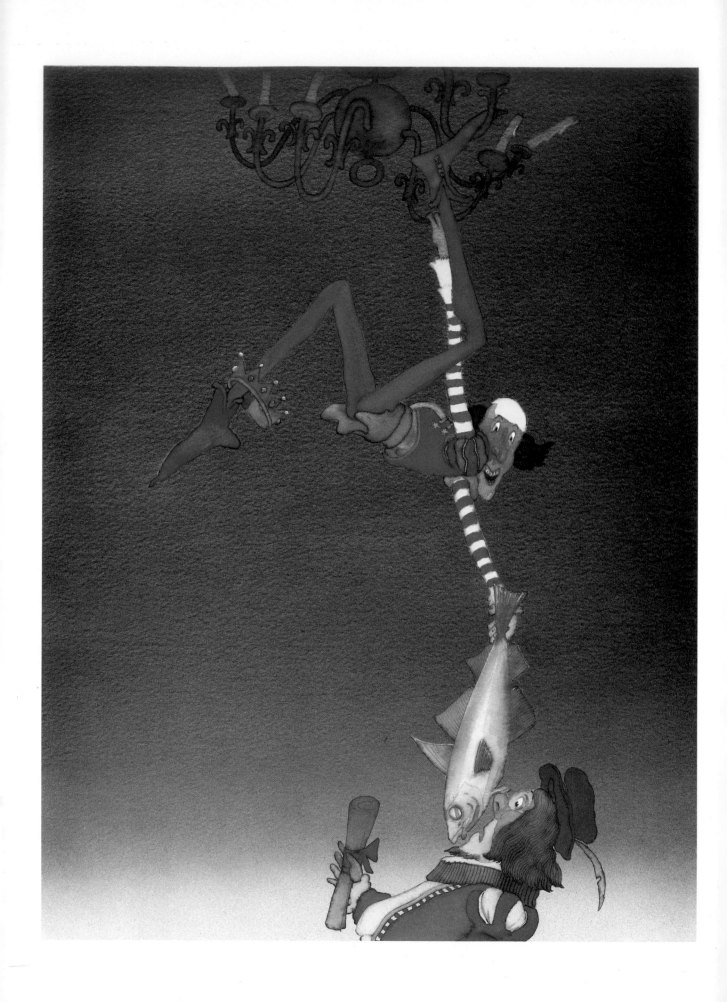

'Oh, King Rupert!' she cried. 'Dreadful news! An army of fifty thousand soldiers is marching through your country!'

King Rupert said: 'Surely that cannot be!' But just then a messenger in King Rupert's own livery rode up on a horse and cried: 'It's true, your Majesty! It's more like a million of them – I've never seen so many!'

King Rupert went deadly pale and fell off his horse in a faint.

They carried him into the throne room, where King Herbert was standing on his head, balancing a box of kippers with his feet. Eventually, King Rupert regained consciousness, and found his son and the Princess looking down at him.

'I am afraid we are homeless now, my dear,' said King Rupert to the Princess. 'An army of fifty million soldiers has overrun our country. Do you think your father will let us stay here to live?'

'Of course he will,' said the Princess. 'Only you mustn't mind if he's a bit silly now and again.'

'Of course not,' said King Rupert, 'we're all a bit silly now and again.'

'That's true,' said the Prince. 'For example, the old lady who stopped you outside the palace was none other than the Princess here, but you didn't recognize her.'

'Indeed I did not,' said King Rupert.

'And the messenger was none other than your own son,' said the Princess, 'and yet you didn't even recognize him.'

'Indeed I did not,' said King Rupert.

'Moreover,' said the Princess, 'you didn't even stop to consider how you could defeat that army of a million soldiers.'

'I have no need to consider it,' said King Rupert. 'How could I possibly deal with an army of such a size?'

'Well, for a start you could pour a kettle of boiling water over them,' said the Princess, 'for they're only an army of soldier ants.'

Whereupon King Rupert laughed out loud at his own silliness, and agreed that the Princess should marry the Prince without delay, and he didn't even mind when King Herbert poured lemonade down his trousers and put ice-cream all over his crown.

The Wonderful Cake-Horse

 MAN ONCE MADE A CAKE shaped like a horse. That night a shooting star flew over the house and a spark happened to fall on the cake-horse. Well, the cake-horse lay there for a few moments. Then it gave a snort. Then it whinnied, scrambled to its legs, and shook its mane of white icing, and stood there in the moonlight, gazing round at the world.

The man, who was asleep in bed, heard the noise and looked out of the window, and saw his cake-horse running around the garden, bucking and snorting, just as if it had been a real wild horse.

'Hey! cake-horse!' cried the man. 'What are you doing?'

'Aren't I a fine horse!' cried the cake-horse. 'You can ride me if you like.'

But the man said: 'You've got no horse-shoes and you've got no saddle, and you're only made of cake!'

The cake-horse snorted and bucked and kicked the air, and galloped across the garden, and leapt clean over the gate, and disappeared into the night.

The next morning, the cake-horse arrived in the nearby town, and went to the blacksmith and said: 'Blacksmith, make me some good horse-shoes, for my feet are only made of cake.'

But the blacksmith said: 'How will you pay me?'

And the cake-horse answered: 'If you make me some horse-shoes, I'll be your friend.'

But the blacksmith shook his head: 'I don't need friends like that!' he said.

So the cake-horse galloped to the saddler, and said: 'Saddler! Make me a saddle of the best leather – one that will go with my icing-sugar mane!'

But the saddler said: 'If I make you a saddle, how will you pay me?'

'I'll be your friend,' said the cake-horse.

'I don't need friends like that!' said the saddler and shook his head.

The cake-horse snorted and bucked and kicked its legs in the air and said: 'Why doesn't anyone want to be my friend? I'll go and join the wild horses!' And he galloped out of the town and off to the moors where the wild horses roamed.

But when he saw the other wild horses, they were all so big and wild that he was afraid they would trample him to crumbs without even noticing he was there.

Just then he came upon a mouse who was groaning to himself under a stone.

'What's the matter with you?' asked the cake-horse.

'Oh,' said the mouse, 'I ran away from my home in the town, and came up here where there is nothing to eat, and now I'm dying of hunger and too weak to get back.'

The cake-horse felt very sorry for the mouse, so it said: 'Here you are! You can nibble a bit of me, if you like, for I'm made of cake.'

'That's most kind of you,' said the mouse, and he ate a little of the cake-horse's tail, and a little of his icing-sugar mane. 'Now I feel much better.'

Then the cake-horse said: 'If only I had a saddle and some horse-shoes, I could carry you back to the town.'

'*I'll* make you them,' said the mouse, and he made four little horse-shoes out of acorn-cups, and a saddle out of beetle-shells, and he got up on the cake-horse's back and rode him back to town.

And there they remained the best of friends for the rest of their lives.

The Fly-By-Night

LITTLE GIRL WAS LYING in bed one night when she heard a tapping on her window. She was rather frightened, but she went to the window and opened it, telling herself that it was probably just the wind. But when she looked out, do you know what she saw? It was a little creature as black as soot, with bright yellow eyes, and it was sitting on a cat that appeared to be flying.

'Hello,' said the creature, 'would you like to come flying?'

'Yes, *please*!' said the little girl, and she climbed out of the window on to the cat and off they flew.

'Hang on tight!' cried the creature.

'Where are we going?' asked the little girl.

'I don't know!' called the creature.

'Who are you?' asked the little girl.

'I haven't got a name,' said the creature, 'I'm just a fly-by-night!' And up they went into the air, over the hills and away.

The little girl looked around her at the bright moon, and the stars that seemed to wink at her and chuckle to themselves. Then she looked down at the black world below her, and she was suddenly frightened again, and said: 'How will we find our way back?'

'Oh! Don't worry about *that*!' cried the fly-by-night. 'What does it matter?' And he leant on the cat's whiskers and down they swooped towards the dark earth.

'But I must be able to get home!' cried the little girl. 'My mother and father will wonder where I am!'

'Oh! Poop-de-doo!' cried the fly-by-night, and he pulled back on the cat's whiskers and up they soared – up and up into the stars again, and all the stars were humming in rhythm:

> Boodle-dum-dee
> Boodle-dum-da,
> Isn't it great,
> Being a star!

And all the stars had hands, and they started clapping together in unison. Then suddenly the Moon opened his mouth and sang in a loud booming voice:

> I'm just the Moon,
> But that's fine by me
> As long as I hear that
> Boodle-dum-dee!

And the cat opened its mouth wide and sang: 'Wheeeeeeee!' and they looped-the-loop and turned circles to the rhythm of the stars.

But the little girl started to cry and said: 'Oh please, I want to go home!'

'Oh no, you don't!' cried the fly-by-night, and took the cat straight up as fast as they could go, and the stars seemed to flash past them like silver darts.

'Please!' cried the little girl. 'Take me back!'

'Spoilsport!' yelled the fly-by-night and he stopped the cat dead, then tipped it over, and down they swooped so fast that they left their stomachs behind them at the top, and landed on a silent hill.

'Here you are!' said the fly-by-night.

'But this isn't my home,' said the little girl, looking around at the dark, lonely countryside.

'Oh! It'll be around somewhere, I expect,' said the fly-by-night.

'But we've come miles and miles from my home!' cried the little girl. But it was too late. The fly-by-night had pulled back on the cat's whiskers and away he soared up into the night sky, and the last the little girl saw of him was a black shape silhouetted against the moon.

The little girl shivered and looked around her, wondering if there were any wild animals about.

'Which way should I go?' she wondered.

'Try the path through the wood,' said a stone at her feet. So she set off along the path that led through the dark wood.

As soon as she got amongst the trees, the leaves blotted out the light of the moon, branches clutched at her hair, and roots tried to trip up her feet, and she thought she heard the trees snigger, quietly; and they seemed to say to each other: 'That'll teach her to go off with a fly-by-night!'

Suddenly she felt a cold hand gripping her neck, but it was just a cobweb strung

with dew. And she heard the spider busy itself with repairs, muttering: 'Tut-tut-tut-tut. She went off with a fly-by-night! Tut-tut-tut-tut.'

As the little girl peered into the wood, she thought she could see eyes watching her and winking to each other and little voices you couldn't really hear whispered under the broad leaves: 'What a silly girl – to go off with a fly-by-night! She should have known better! Tut-tut-tut-tut.'

Eventually she felt so miserable and so foolish that she just sat down and cried by a still pond.

'Now then, what's the matter?' said a kindly voice.

The little girl looked up, and then all around her, but she couldn't see anyone. 'Who's that?' she asked.

'Look in the pond,' said the voice, and she looked down and saw the reflection of the moon, smiling up at her out of the pond.

'Don't take on so,' said the moon.

'But I've been so silly,' said the little girl, 'and now I'm quite, quite lost and I don't know how I'll *ever* get home.'

'You'll get home all right,' said the moon's reflection. 'Hop on a lily-pad and follow me.'

So the little girl stepped cautiously on to a lily-pad, and the moon's reflection started to move slowly across the pond, and then down a stream, and the little girl paddled the lily-pad after it.

Slowly and silently they slipped through the night forest, and then out into the open fields they followed the stream, until they came to a hill she recognized, and suddenly there was her own house. She ran as fast as she could and climbed in through the window of her own room, and snuggled into her own dear bed.

And the moon smiled in at her through the window, and she fell asleep thinking how silly she'd been to go off with the fly-by-night. But, you know, somewhere, deep down inside her, she half-hoped she'd hear another tap on her window one day, and find another fly-by-night offering her a ride on its flying cat.

But she never did.

Three Raindrops

 RAINDROP WAS FALLING out of a cloud, and it said to the raindrop next to it: 'I'm the biggest and best raindrop in the whole sky!'

'You are indeed a fine raindrop,' said the second, 'but you are not nearly so beautifully shaped as I am. And in my opinion it's shape that counts, and *I* am therefore the best raindrop in the whole sky.'

The first raindrop replied: 'Let us settle this matter once and for all.' So they asked a third raindrop to decide between them.

But the third raindrop said: 'What nonsense you're both talking! *You* may be a big raindrop, and *you* are certainly well-shaped, but, as everybody knows, it's purity that really counts, and I am purer than either of you. *I* am therefore the best raindrop in the whole sky!'

Well, before either of the other raindrops could reply, they all three hit the ground and became part of a very muddy puddle.

The Butterfly Who Sang

**A** BUTTERFLY WAS ONCE SITTING ON A LEAF looking extremely sad.

'What's wrong?' asked a friendly frog.

'Oh,' said the butterfly, 'nobody really appreciates me,' and she parted her beautiful red and blue wings and shut them again.

'What d'you mean?' asked the frog. 'I've seen you flying about and thought to myself: that is one hell of a beautiful butterfly! All my friends think you look great, too! You're a real stunner!'

'Oh *that*,' replied the butterfly, and she opened her wings again. 'Who cares about *looks*? It's my singing that nobody appreciates.'

'I've never heard your singing; but if it's anywhere near as good as your looks, you've got it made!' said the frog.

'That's the trouble,' replied the butterfly, 'people say they can't hear my singing. I suppose it's so refined and so high that their ears aren't sensitive enough to pick it up.'

'But I bet it's great all the same!' said the frog.

'It is,' said the butterfly. 'Would you like me to sing for you?'

'Well . . . I don't suppose my ears are sensitive enough to pick it up, but I'll give it a try!' said the frog.

So the butterfly spread her wings, and opened her mouth. The frog gazed in wonder at the butterfly's beautiful wings, for he'd never been so close to them before.

The butterfly sang on and on, and still the frog gazed at her wings, absolutely captivated, even though he could hear nothing whatsoever of her singing.

Eventually, however, the butterfly stopped, and closed up her wings.

'Beautiful!' said the frog, thinking about the wings.

'Thank you,' said the butterfly, thrilled that at last she had found an appreciative listener.

After that, the frog came every day to listen to the butterfly sing, though all the time he was really feasting his eyes on her beautiful wings. And every day, the butterfly tried harder and harder to impress the frog with her singing, even though he could not hear a single note of it.

But one day a moth, who was jealous of all the attention the butterfly was getting, took the butterfly on one side and said: 'Butterfly, your singing is quite superb.'

'Thank you,' said the butterfly.

'With just a little more practice,' said the cunning moth, 'you could be as famous a singer as the nightingale.'

'Do you think so?' asked the butterfly, flattered beyond words.

'I certainly do,' replied the moth. 'Indeed, perhaps you already *do* sing better than the nightingale, only it's difficult to concentrate on your music because your gaudy wings are so distracting.'

'Is that right?' said the butterfly.

'I'm afraid so,' said the moth. 'You notice the nightingale is wiser, and wears only dull brown feathers so as not to distract from her singing.'

'You're right!' cried the butterfly. 'I was a fool not to have realized that before!' And straight away she found some earth and rubbed it into her wings until they were all grey and half the colours had rubbed off.

The next day, the frog arrived for the concert as usual, but when the butterfly opened her wings he cried out: 'Oh! Butterfly! What have you done to your beautiful wings?' And the butterfly explained what she had done.

'I think you will find', she said, 'that now you will be able to concentrate more on my music.'

Well, the poor frog tried, but it was no good, for of course he couldn't hear anything at all. So he soon became bored, and hopped off into the pond. And after that the butterfly never *could* find anyone to listen to her singing.

Jack One-Step

 BOY NAMED JACK WAS ON HIS WAY to school, when he heard a tapping noise coming from an old log. He bent down and put his ear to the log. Sure enough, it sounded as if there was something inside it. And then he heard a tiny voice calling out: 'Help! Please help!'

'Who's that?' asked Jack.

'Please,' said the voice, 'my name is Fairy One-Step, and I was sleeping in this old hollow log when it rolled over and trapped me inside.'

'If you're a fairy,' said Jack, 'why don't you just do some magic and escape?'

There was a slight pause, and then Jack heard a little sigh and the voice said: 'I wish I could, but I'm only a very small fairy and I can only do one spell.'

So Jack turned the log over and, sure enough, a little creature the size of his big toe hopped out and gave him a bow.

'Thank you,' said the fairy. 'I would like to do something for you in return.'

'Well,' said Jack, 'since you *are* a fairy, how about granting me three wishes?'

The fairy hung his head and replied: 'I'm afraid I haven't the magic to do that – I'm only a very small fairy, you see, and I only have one spell.'

'What is that?' asked Jack.

'I can grant you one step that will take you wherever you want to go,' said the fairy.

'Would I be able to take one step from here to that tree over there?' asked Jack.

'Oh – farther than that!' said the fairy.

'Would I be able to take one step all the way home?' asked Jack.

'Farther, if you wanted,' said the fairy.

'You mean I could take one step and get as far as London?' gasped Jack.

'You could take your one step right across the ocean, if you wanted – or even to the moon. Would you like that?'

'Yes, *please*!' said Jack.

So Fairy One-Step did the spell and Jack felt a sort of tingle go down his legs. Then the fairy said: 'Now *do* think carefully where you want to go.'

'I will,' said Jack. Then he thought for a bit, and asked: 'If I have only one step, how do I get back again?'

Fairy One-Step went a little red and hung his head again and replied: 'That's the snag. If *only* I wasn't such a small fairy.' And with that he flew off, and Jack went on his way to school.

All that day he hardly listened to what his teacher said, he was so busy thinking of where he would like to step to.

'I'd like to go to Africa,' he thought, 'but how would I get back? I'd like to go to the North Pole, but I'd be stuck there. . . .' And try as he might, he *couldn't* think of anywhere that he wouldn't want to get back from.

That night, he couldn't sleep for thinking but, the next morning, he leapt out of bed and said: 'I know where I'll go!'

He went out of the house and said aloud: 'I'll take my step to where the King of the Fairies lives.' As soon as he'd said it, he felt a tingle down his legs, and he took a step and found himself rising into the air. Up and up he went, above the trees, higher and higher, and, when he looked back, his home was like a doll's house on the earth below, and he could see his mother waving frantically up at him. Jack

waved back, but he felt his step taking him on and on, over hills and valleys and
forests, and soon he found himself over the ocean, going so fast that the wind
whistled past his ears. On and on he went, until in the distance he could see a land
with high mountains that sparkled as if they were made of cut-glass. And he found
himself coming down from the clouds . . . and down . . . until he landed in a green
valley at the foot of the cut-glass mountains. And there on a hill up above him was
a white castle with towers and turrets that reached up into the sky. From it he could
hear strange music, and he knew that this must be the castle where the King of the
Fairies lived.

There was a path leading up the hill to the castle, so he set off along it. Well, he
hadn't gone more than a couple of steps when a cloud of smoke appeared in front of
him. When it cleared away, he found himself staring straight into the eyes of a huge
dragon that was breathing fire out of its nostrils.

'Where do you think you're going?' asked the dragon.

'To see the King of the Fairies,' replied Jack.

'Huh!' replied the dragon, and breathed a long jet of flame that set fire to a tree.
'Go back where you came from.'

'I can't,' replied Jack. 'I came by one magic step and I haven't got another.'

'In that case,' said the dragon, 'I shall have to burn you up.'

But Jack was too quick for him. He sprang behind the dragon's back, and the
dragon span round so fast that it set fire to its own tail, and Jack left it trying to put
out the flames by rolling in the grass.

Jack ran as hard as he could, right up to the door of the castle, and rang the great
bell. Immediately the door flew open and an ogre with hair all over his face looked
out and said: 'You'd better go back where you came from or I'll cut you up into
pieces and feed them to my dog.'

'Please,' said Jack, 'I can't go back. I came by one magic step and I haven't got
another. I've come to see the King of the Fairies.'

'The King of the Fairies is too busy,' said the ogre, and pulled out his sword that
was six times as long as Jack himself. And the ogre held it over his head and was just
about to bring it down, when Jack jumped up and pushed the ogre's beard up his

nose. And the ogre gave a terrible sneeze and brought down his sword and cut off his own leg.

Jack dashed inside, and shut the door. The castle was very dark, but in the distance Jack could still hear the fairy music that he had heard before. So he crept through corridors and down passageways, expecting at any moment to meet another monster. He found himself walking past deep black holes in the wall, from which he could hear horrible grunts and the chink of chains, and he could smell brimstone and the stench of scaly animals. Sometimes he would come to deep chasms in the floor of the castle, and find himself looking down thousands of feet into seething waters below, and the only way across was a narrow bridge of brick no wider than his shoe. But he kept on towards the fairy music, and at length he saw a light at the end of the passage.

When he reached the door, he found himself standing in the great hall of the Fairy King. There were lights everywhere, and the walls were mirrors so that a thousand reflections greeted his gaze and he could not tell how large the hall really was. The fairies were all in the middle of a dance, but they stopped as soon as they saw him. The music ceased, and at the end of the hall sat the King of the Fairies himself. He was huge and had great bulging eyes and a fierce beard and a ring in his ear.

'Who is this?' he cried. 'Who dares to interrupt our celebration?'

Jack felt very frightened, for he could feel the power of magic hovering in the air, and all those fairy eyes, wide and cold, staring at him.

'Please,' said Jack, 'I've come to complain.'

'Complain!' roared the King of the Fairies, turning first blue and then green with rage. '*No-one* dares to complain to the King of the Fairies!'

'Well,' said Jack, as bravely as he could, trying to ignore all those glittering fairy eyes, 'I think it's most unfair to leave Fairy One-Step with only one spell – and that not a very good one.'

'Fairy One-Step's only a very small fairy!' bellowed the King of the Fairies, and he stood up and he towered above all the other fairies. Then he held his hands in the air, and everything went deathly silent.

Jack felt even more frightened, but he stood there bravely and said: 'You ought to be ashamed of yourself. Just because you're the biggest of the fairies, that's no reason to treat the small ones badly.'

Well, the King of the Fairies went first green then purple then black with anger. But just then a little voice at Jack's elbow said: 'He's right!' and Jack looked down and found Fairy One-Step standing by him.

Then another voice at the other end of the hall said: 'That's true! Why should small fairies be worse off than big fairies?'

And suddenly another fairy said: 'Why?' and soon all the fairies were shouting out: 'Yes! *Why*?'

The King of the Fairies drew himself up, and looked fearfully angry and roared: 'Because I'm more powerful than *any* of you!' and he raised his hands to cast a spell.

But the fairies called out: 'But you're not more powerful than *all* of us!' and do you know what happened then? In a flash, all the other fairies disappeared and, before he could stop himself, the King of the Fairies had cast his spell right at his own reflection in one of the mirrors. The King of the Fairies shook and trembled, and first his beard fell off, then he shrank to half his size and fell on all fours and turned into a wild boar and went charging about the hall of mirrors.

Then the other fairies reappeared, and threw him out of the castle. And they made Fairy One-Step their King, and granted Jack one more magic step to take him home.

And that's just where he went.

The Glass Cupboard

HERE WAS ONCE A CUPBOARD that was made entirely of glass so you could see right into it and right through it. Now, although this cupboard always appeared to be empty, you could always take out whatever you wanted. If you wanted a cool drink, for example, you just opened the cupboard and took one out. Or if you wanted a new pair of shoes, you could always take a pair out of the glass cupboard. Even if you wanted a bag of gold, you just opened up the glass cupboard and took out a bag of gold. The only thing you had to remember was that, whenever you took something *out* of the glass cupboard, you had to put something else back *in*, although nobody quite knew why.

Naturally such a valuable thing as the glass cupboard belonged to a rich and powerful King.

One day, the King had to go on a long journey, and while he was gone some thieves broke into the palace and stole the glass cupboard.

'Now we can have anything we want,' they said.

One of the robbers said: 'I want a large bag of gold,' and he opened the glass cupboard and took out a large bag of gold.

Then the second robber said: 'I want two large bags of gold,' and he opened the glass cupboard and took out two large bags of gold.

Then the chief of the robbers said: 'I want three of the biggest bags of gold you've ever seen!' and he opened the glass cupboard and took out three of the biggest bags of gold you've ever seen.

'Hooray!' they said. 'Now we can take out as much gold as we like!'

Well, those three robbers stayed up the whole night, taking bag after bag of gold out of the glass cupboard. But not one of them put anything back in.

In the morning, the chief of the robbers said: 'Soon we shall be the richest three men in the world. But let us go to sleep now, and we can take out more gold tonight.'

So they lay down to sleep. But the first robber could not sleep. He kept thinking: 'If I went to the glass cupboard just *once* more, I'd be even richer than I am now.' So he got up, and went to the cupboard, and took out yet another bag of gold, and then went back to bed.

And the second robber could not sleep either. He kept thinking: 'If I went to the glass cupboard and took out two more bags of gold, I'd be even richer than the others.' So he got up, and went to the cupboard, and took out two more bags of gold, and then went back to bed.

Meanwhile the chief of the robbers could not sleep either. He kept thinking: 'If I went to the glass cupboard and took out three more bags of gold, I'd be the richest of all.' So he got up, and went to the cupboard, and took out three more bags of gold, and then went back to bed.

And then the first robber said to himself: 'What am I doing, lying here sleeping, when I could be getting richer?' So he got up, and started taking more and more bags of gold out of the cupboard.

The second robber heard him and thought: 'What am I doing, lying here sleeping, when he's getting richer than me?' So he got up and joined his companion.

And then the chief of the robbers got up too. 'I can't lie here sleeping,' he said, 'while the other two are both getting richer than me.' So he got up and soon all three were hard at it, taking more and more bags of gold out of the cupboard.

And all that day and all that night not one of them dared to stop for fear that one of his companions would get richer than him. And they carried on all the next day and all the next night. They didn't stop to rest, and they didn't stop to eat, and they didn't even stop to drink. They kept taking out those bags of gold faster and faster

35

and more and more until, at length, they grew faint with lack of sleep and food and drink, but still they did not dare to stop.

All that week and all the next week, and all that month and all that winter, they kept at it, until the chief of the robbers could bear it no longer, and he picked up a hammer and smashed the glass cupboard into a million pieces, and they all three gave a great cry and fell down dead on top of the huge mountain of gold they had taken out of the glass cupboard.

Sometime later the King returned home, and his servants threw themselves on their knees before him, and said: 'Forgive us, Your Majesty, but three wicked robbers have stolen the glass cupboard!'

The King ordered his servants to search the length and breadth of the land. When they found what was left of the glass cupboard, and the three robbers lying dead, they filled sixty great carts with all the gold and took it back to the King. And when the King heard that the glass cupboard was smashed into a million pieces and that the three thieves were dead, he shook his head and said: 'If those thieves had always put something back into the cupboard for every bag of gold they had taken out, they would be alive to this day.' And he ordered his servants to collect all the pieces of the glass cupboard and to melt them down and make them into a globe with all the countries of the world upon it, to remind himself, and others, that the earth is as fragile as that glass cupboard.

Katy-Make-Sure

THERE WAS ONCE A LITTLE GIRL called Katy, who found an old shoe inside a hollow tree. It was a funny little shoe with a pointed toe and it was no more than an inch long.

'I wonder who it can belong to?' she thought, and she slipped it into the pocket of her dress, and went on her way. She hadn't gone very far before she heard a sound like this:

> tippity-tap
> tippity-tap
> tippity-tap

She looked round a large oak tree and saw a little goblin hopping around on one foot. 'Excuse me,' she said, 'but is this your shoe?'

Well, the goblin danced for joy.

'At last!' he cried. 'Without my shoes I can't go back to Goblin City.'

So Katy gave the goblin his shoe, and he put it on, and danced around the tree, singing:

> Short or long to Goblin City?
> The straight way's short,
> But the long way's pretty!

Then he stopped, and said to Katy: 'If you come with me to Goblin City, the King of the Goblins will give you a reward.'

'Well, I *could* come,' said Katy, 'but how would we get there?'
The goblin just hopped up and down on one leg and chanted:

> Short or long to Goblin City?
> The straight way's short,
> But the long way's pretty!

'But how do I know if it's worth going the pretty way, or if it'll take too long?' asked Katy.

The goblin jumped in the air, twirled round three times before he landed on one toe, and said:

> Short or long to Goblin City?
> The straight way's short,
> But the long way's pretty!

'How can I be sure it's not better to go the short way?' asked Katy.

The goblin jumped in the air, landed on his head, and span round and round like a top until he disappeared into the ground, and then reappeared just behind Katy and cried:

> Short or long to Goblin City?
> The straight way's short,
> But the long way's pretty!

'How can I be sure I'll like it, whichever way we go?' asked Katy.

The goblin did a somersault, and landed on one finger. Then he snapped his finger so hard that he rose into the air, up and up, and then came tumbling down and landed in a dandelion puff-ball, and cried:

> Goblin City's far and near!
> If you want to make sure,
> You'd better stay here!

With that, a puff of wind caught the dandelion and scattered it to the four corners of the world, and the goblin was gone too.

And poor Katy never went to Goblin City either way.

The Wooden City

THERE WAS ONCE A POOR KING. He had a threadbare robe and patches on his throne. The reason he was poor was that he gave away all his money to whomever needed it, for he cared for his people as if each of them was his own child.

One day, however, a wizard came to the city while the King was away. The wizard summoned all the people into the main square, and said to them: 'Make me your king, and you shall have all the gold and silver you ever wanted!'

Now the townsfolk talked amongst themselves and said: 'Our King is poor, for he has given all his money away, and while it is certainly true that there are no beggars in this kingdom, it is also true that none of us are very rich nor can expect to be as long as our present King reigns.' So at length they agreed that the Wizard should become their king.

'And will you obey my laws – whatever I decree?' cried the Wizard.

'If we can have all the gold and silver we ever wanted,' they replied, 'you may make what laws you wish.'

Whereupon the Wizard climbed to the top of the tallest tower in the city. He took a live dove, and tore out its feathers, and dropped them one by one out of the tower, chanting:

> Gold and silver shall be yours
> And blocks of wood shall serve my laws.

Now that poor dove had as many feathers on its back as there were people in that city and, by the time the wizard had finished, everyone in the city had been turned to wood.

When the King arrived back, he found the gates of the city shut and no-one to open them. So he sent his servant to find out what was the matter. The servant returned, saying he could not find the gatekeeper, but only a wooden mannequin dressed in the gatekeeper's uniform, standing in his place.

At length, however, the gates were opened, and the King went into the city. But instead of cheering crowds, he found only wooden people, each standing where

40

they had been when the wizard cast his spell. There was a wooden shoemaker sitting working at a pair of new shoes. Outside the inn was a wooden innkeeper, pouring some beer from a jug into the cup of a wooden old man. Wooden women were hanging blankets out of the windows, or walking wooden children down the street. And at the fish shop, a wooden fishmonger stood by a slab of rotten fish. And when the King entered his palace, he even found his own wife and children turned to wood. Filled with despair, he sat down on the floor and wept.

Whereupon the Wizard appeared, and said to the King: 'Will you become my slave if I bring your people back to life?'

And the King answered : 'Nothing would be too much to ask. I would become your slave.'

So the wizard set to work. He ordered a quantity of the finest wood, and took the most delicate tools, with golden screws and silver pins, and he made a little wooden heart that beat and pumped for everyone in that city. Then he placed one heart inside each of the wooden citizens, and set it working.

One by one, each citizen opened its wooden eyes, and looked stiffly around, while its wooden heart beat: tunca-tunca-tunca. Then each wooden citizen moved a wooden leg and a wooden arm, and then one by one they started to go about their business as before, except stiffly and awkwardly, for they were still made of wood.

Then the Wizard appeared before the King and said: 'Now you are my slave!'

'But', cried the King, 'my people are still made of wood, you have not *truly* brought them back to life.'

'Enough life to work for me!' cried the wicked old wizard. And he ordered the wooden army to throw the King out of the city and bolt the gates.

The King wandered through the world, begging for his food, and seeking someone who could bring his subjects back to life. But he could find no-one. In

41

despair, he took work as a shepherd, minding sheep on a hill that overlooked the city, and there he would often stop travellers as they passed to and fro and ask them how it was in the great city.

'It's fine,' they would reply, 'the citizens make wonderful clocks and magnificent clothes woven out of precious metals, and they sell these things cheaper than anywhere else on earth!'

One night, however, the King determined to see how things were for himself. So he crept down to the walls, and climbed in through a secret window, and went to the main square. There an extraordinary sight met his eyes. Although it was the dead of night, every one of those wooden citizens was working as if it had been broad daylight. None of them spoke a word, however, and the only sound was the tunca-tunca-tunca of their wooden hearts beating in their wooden chests.

The King ran from one to the other saying: 'Don't you remember me? I am your King.' But they all just stared at him blankly and then hurried on their way.

At length the King saw his own daughter coming down the street carrying a load of firewood for the wizard's fire. He caught hold of her and lifted her up and said: 'Daughter! Don't you remember me? Don't you remember you're a Princess?'

But his daughter looked at him and said: 'I remember nothing, but I have gold and silver in my purse.'

So the King leapt on to a box in the main square and cried out: 'You are all under the wizard's spell! Help me seize him and cast him out!'

But they all turned with blank faces and replied: 'We have all the gold and silver we ever wanted. Why should we do anything?'

Just then, the wizard himself appeared on the steps of the palace, arrayed in a magnificent robe of gold and silver, and carrying a flaming torch.

'Ah ha!' he cried. 'So you thought you'd undo my work, did you? Very well . . . .' And he raised his hands to cast a spell upon the King. But before he could utter a single word, the King seized the bundle of firewood that his daughter was carrying and hurled it at the wizard. At once the flame from the wizard's torch caught the wood, and the blazing pieces fell down around him in a circle of fire that swallowed him up. And as the fire raged, the spell began to lift.

The King's daughter and all the others shivered, and the tunca-tunca-tunca of their wooden hearts changed to real heartbeats, and they each turned back into flesh and blood. And when they looked where the wizard had been, there in his place they found a molten heap of twisted gold and silver. This, the King had raised up on a pedestal in the main square, and underneath he had written the words:

'Whoever needs gold or silver may take from here.'

But, do you know, not one of those townsfolk ever took a single scrap of it as long as they lived.

I wonder if it's still there?

The Ship of Bones

IN THE DAYS WHEN SAILING SHIPS crossed the oceans, blown by the winds, there was one ship that all sailors dreaded to see. It was called the Ship of Bones. Its sails were deathly white and its figurehead was a skull and all along its length were carved the names of drowned sailors, and they say that the hull was made from their bones.

This is the story of the only man who went aboard the Ship of Bones and lived to tell the tale. His name was Stoker, Bill Stoker, and he sailed on the ship *Mayfly*, that left Portsmouth on 1 June 1784. . . .

They hadn't been gone more than a week when they were caught in a storm . . . in a terrible storm. The waves towered up six times as high as the mainmast, and the little ship was tossed about the ocean like a bit of cork in the foam. One moment it was rising up the head of a mighty wave and the next minute it was dashed down into the trough, and the waters blotted out the sun and it all went still, until another wave crashed down on her bows.

Well, the storm raged on for four days and four nights, and on the fourth night the sailors had given themselves up as good as dead. Their sails were in shreds, the rudder was broken, and half the crew were lying sick in their hammocks or being tossed across the cabin by the force of the sea.

Old Bill Stoker was lying in his bunk, thinking this would be his last night on this earth, when he heard a cry from up on deck, and this sailor comes running down to the cabin as white as a sheet.

'It's the Ship of Bones!' he cries. 'We've had it now for sure, mates!'

Now old Bill Stoker was not one to take things lying down. 'I don't believe in no Ship of Bones,' he says, and leaps out of his bunk and climbs up on deck.

It was dreadful night. The rain lashed across his face, and the wind was blowing up the sea like so many mountains. Bill Stoker peers into the storm, and – sure enough – across the tops of the raging waters he can just make out the whitest ship you ever saw. Its sails were almost glowing white in the darkness.

'Well!' shouts Bill Stoker. 'If that's the Ship of Bones, I'll eat my hat!'

Just then, a mighty wave smashes across the deck and, before he knows what's hit him, Bill Stoker finds himself lifted high up in the air on top of the wave. He looks down and there – a hundred feet below – is his own ship. Then suddenly, he's thrown through the air by the force of the wave, and he lands slap in the middle of another, and he goes right under. Well, just as he's beginning to gasp for breath, he finds himself shooting out and up into the air again on another monstrous wave. And this time he looks down, and just catches sight of the white ship below him, when he finds himself hurtling downwards again. Then everything goes deathly quiet and still.

Well, he opens his eyes and looks around. Sure enough he's lying right there on the deck of the Ship of Bones. He can see the black night and the storm raging all about. But the ship itself is quite still – scarcely moving, like, as if it were becalmed. And there's not a sound.

Bill Stoker puts his hand out and feels the deck. It's smooth like ivory and, even though the rain and the waves are lashing the ship, the deck itself is quite, quite dry. Well, Bill looks around and sees that he's all alone, except for an old sailor who's winding in the anchor. So he gets to his feet and calls out: 'Ahoy there!' But the old sailor doesn't turn round – he just keeps on a-winding in that anchor. So Bill Stoker walks across the deck and says: 'Ahoy there, matey! What's to do?'

The old sailor turns round, and do you know? He hasn't got a face – leastwise, not what you'd *call* a face – more of a skull . . . . And his hands are skeleton hands. And his jaws open and a cracked voice says: 'Welcome to the Ship of Bones, Bill!' And he puts out a boney hand to take hold of Bill Stoker. But old Bill Stoker – he backs away. Then he turns on his heels and runs as hard as he can, and ducks below decks. But he can hear the skeleton coming after him, so he shuts the hatch and skids down those steps as fast as he can.

Inside the ship there's a curious smell, like you get around tombstones. Bill Stoker grabs the rail as he goes down, and he notices that everything's made out of bones – white and yellow, old and new. But he can still hear the skeleton footsteps coming after him, so he goes right on down into the hold.

It's so dark, he can't see for a bit . . . then suddenly he hears a shout: 'Why! Here's Bill Stoker! Hello there, Bill! Welcome to the Ship of Bones!'

Bill's eyes are used to the dark by now, and he can just see some shapes rising up off their beds and coming towards him. Well! He doesn't stop to see who they are: he doubles back on himself and runs back up the steps. And there's the skeleton sailor, standing at the top, grinning down at him.

Well, old Bill Stoker wasn't a man to be scared easily, so he runs up the steps, gets out his cutlass and strikes at the creature. But the skeleton sailor hops out of the way, and grabs Bill's shirt as he runs past. But it's an old shirt, and it rips apart before the thing can get its boney fingers over Bill's throat. In a trice, Bill's up on deck again, sprinting across to the bridge house.

Once inside, he locks the door . . . but he can hear the boney steps coming nearer and nearer. Then he sees that horrible grinning skull's face, leering in at the window.

Bill wasn't a man to give up, like, so he thinks to himself: 'They're just a lot of old bones – all of them – they must be scared of *something*.' Then he gets an idea. 'I know what'll see old bones off!' he cries, and he drops down on all fours and starts barking like a dog. Well, the skull's face sort of frowns. Old Bill flings the door open and leaps out – barking like mad. And do you know? That horrible creature just turns and runs. Whereupon old Bill takes his chance, and leaps over the side. Immediately he feels the waves picking him up and flinging him across the water again. . . .

Well, I don't know what happened next, and I don't think old Bill knew, but he finally found himself back on his own boat, with his shipmates all standing around him and pointing. And Bill looked out into the night and he saw that Ship of Bones going off as fast as it could – to wherever it came from.

Not long after that, the storm died down, and they came out into calmer waters, and old Bill Stoker told his story to his shipmates, and they all listened with bated breath. But do you know? Not one of them believed it. But that didn't worry old Bill Stoker. And that evening he sat right down and – can you guess what he did? He *ate his hat*!

47

Simple Peter's Mirror

SIMPLE PETER WAS WALKING TO WORK in the fields one morning when he met an old woman sitting beside the road.

'Good morning, old woman,' he said, 'why do you look so sad?'

'I have lost my ring,' said the old woman, 'and it is the only one like it in the whole world.'

'I will help you find it,' said Simple Peter, and he got down on his hands and knees to look for the old woman's ring.

Well, he hunted for a long time, until at last he found the ring under a leaf.

'Thank you,' said the old woman. 'That ring is more precious than you realize,' and she slipped it on to her finger. Then she took a mirror out of her apron and gave it to Peter, saying: 'Take this as a reward.'

Now Simple Peter had never seen a mirror before and so, when he looked down and saw the reflection of the sky in his hands, he said: 'Have you given me the sky?'

'No,' said the old woman, and explained what it was.

'What do I want with a mirror?' asked Peter.

'That is no ordinary mirror,' replied the old woman. 'It is a magic mirror. Anyone who looks into it will see themselves not as they are, but as other people see them. And that's a great gift, you know, to see ourselves as others see us.'

Simple Peter held the mirror up to his face and peered into it. First he turned one way, then he turned the other. He held the mirror sideways and longways and upside down, and finally he shook his head and said: 'Well, it may be a magic mirror, but it's no good to me, I can't see myself in it at all.'

The old woman smiled and said: 'The mirror will never lie to you. It will show you a true reflection of yourself as other people see you.' And with that she touched her ring, and the oak tree that was standing behind her bent down and picked her

up in its branches, and carried her away.

Well, Simple Peter stood there gaping for a long while, and then he looked in the mirror again, and still he could not see himself, even when he put his nose right up against it.

Just then a farmer came riding past on his way to market. 'Excuse me,' said Simple Peter, 'but have you seen my reflection? I can't find it in this mirror.'

'Oh,' said the farmer, 'I saw it half an hour ago, running down the road.'

'Thank you,' said Peter, 'I'll see if I can catch it,' and he ran off down the road.

The farmer laughed and said to himself: 'That Simple Peter is a proper goose!' and he went on his way.

Simple Peter ran on and on until he came to the blacksmith.

'Where are you running so fast, Peter?' called the blacksmith.

'I'm trying to catch my reflection,' replied Peter. 'John the farmer said it ran this way. Did you see it?'

The blacksmith, who was a kindly man, shook his head and said: 'John the farmer has been telling you stories. Your reflection can't run away from you. Look in the mirror, and you'll see it there all right.'

So Peter looked in the magic mirror, and do you know what he saw? He saw a goose, with a yellow beak and black eyes, staring straight back at him.

'There, do you see your reflection?' asked the blacksmith.

'I only see a goose,' said Peter, 'but *I'm* not a goose. I'll show you all! I'll seek my fortune, and then you'll see me as I really am!'

So Peter set off to seek his fortune.

Before long, he came to a wild place in the mountains, where he met a woodcutter and his family with all their belongings on their backs.

'Where are you going?' he asked them.

'We're leaving this country,' said the woodcutter, 'because there is a dragon here. It is fifty times as big as a man and could eat you up in one mouthful. Now it has carried off the King's daughter and is going to eat her for supper tonight.' And with that they hurried on their way.

Peter went on, and the mountains grew steeper and the way became harder. All at once he heard a sound like a grindstone. He looked round a rock and there he saw the dragon. Sure enough, it was fifty times as big as himself and it was spinning a stone round in its front claws to sharpen its teeth.

'Oh ho! Are you the dragon?' asked Peter. The dragon stopped sharpening its teeth and glared with great fierce eyes at Peter.

'I am!' said the dragon.

'Then I shall have to kill you,' said Peter.

'*Indeed?*' said the dragon, and the spines on its back started to bristle, and tongues of flame began to leap out of its nostrils. 'And how are *you* going to kill *me?*'

And Peter said: 'Oh, *I'm* not, but behind this rock I have the most terrible creature, that is fifty times as big as you, and could eat *you* up in one mouthful!'

'Impossible!' roared the dragon, and leapt behind the rock. Now Peter, who was not *so* simple after all, had hidden the magic mirror there, and so when the dragon came leaping round the rock it ran slap bang into it, and there, for the first time, it saw itself as it appeared to others – fifty times as big and able to eat itself up in one mouthful! And then and there that dragon turned on its tail and ran off over the mountains as fast as it could, and was never seen again.

Then Peter went into the dragon's cave, and found the King's daughter, and carried her back to the palace. And the King gave him jewels and fine clothes and all the people cheered him to the skies. And when Peter looked in the magic mirror now, do you know what he saw? He saw himself as a brave, fierce lion, which was how everyone else saw him. But he said to himself: 'I'm not a lion! I'm Peter.'

Just then the Princess came by and Peter showed her the mirror and asked her what she saw there.

'I see the most beautiful girl in the world,' said the Princess. 'But *I'm* not the most beautiful girl in the world.'

'But that's how you appear to me,' said Peter, and he told the Princess the whole story about how he had come by the mirror, and how he had tricked the dragon.

'So you see, I'm not really a goose, and I'm not really as brave as a lion. I'm just Simple Peter.'

When the Princess heard his story, she began to like him for his straightforwardness and honesty. Pretty soon she grew to love him, and the King

agreed that they should be married, even though Peter was just a poor ploughman's son.

'But, my dear!' said the Queen. 'People will make fun of us because he is not a real prince.'

'Fiddlesticks!' replied the King. 'We'll make him into the finest prince you ever did see!' But the old Queen was right. . . .

On the day of the wedding, Peter was dressed up in the finest clothes, trimmed with gold and fur. But when he looked in the magic mirror, do you know what he saw? Instead of a rich and magnificent prince, he saw himself in his own rags – Simple Peter. But it didn't worry him. He smiled and said to himself: 'At last! Everyone sees me as I really am!'

Brave Molly

A LITTLE GIRL WAS ONCE CAUGHT IN A THUNDERSTORM. The day grew dark, and the wind started to blow, and suddenly a fork of lightning streaked across the sky and a great clap of thunder rolled all around her. Poor Molly trembled with fright, and she wished she were back at home with her mother. Then it started to rain. Such a cloudburst it was! The heavens just opened up and down came the rain in great big drops the size of your fist.

In the distance, Molly could see a little hut, so she ran up to it and, finding the door open, she slipped into the gloomy inside. No sooner had she shut the door than a deep growling voice said: 'Grrrrr! Who are you?'

Molly looked around her, but the inside of the hut was quite dark, and she couldn't see anyone.

'P-p-p-please . . . my name's M-M-M-Molly,' she said. 'Who are you?'

'Grrrrr! I'm a Terrible Monster – that's who!' said the voice.

Just then a bolt of lightning lit up the inside of the hut for a fraction of a second and, in that moment, Molly saw a huge black shape crouching against the far end of the hut. 'Ohhhhh!' she cried.

'What's the matter?' growled the Terrible Monster. 'Frightened, are you?'

'Indeed I am,' said Molly. 'You're as black as coal, as big as a house and covered in hair.'

'And I've got a terrible roar,' said the Monster. 'AAAAAAAA-RRRRRRRRGH!'

Poor Molly fell over backwards in her fright. And the thunder crashed over their heads, and another flash of lightning lit up the Monster, and Molly could see that he had great black claws and glowing eyes and huge yellow teeth.

'Pretty frightening, huh?' bellowed the Monster.

'Oh y-y-y-yes!' cried Molly.

'*And* I'm as strong as two hundred oxen!' he cried and, as the lightning flashed, Molly saw the Monster rear up on his legs and throw the roof of the hut high into the air.

'Oh . . . please don't!' cried Molly, as the rain started to pour down on her and the thunder crashed.

'*And* I eat little girls for my supper!' roared the Monster. And he bent down and put one glowing eye right up against poor Molly, and said: 'How about *that*?'

'Well,' Molly thought to herself, 'it's no use being frightened. If he's going to eat me – he's going to eat me.' So she picked up her satchel and hit that Monster right on the nose. And do you know what happened? Well, the Monster didn't pick her up in his huge claws, and he didn't gobble her up with his great yellow teeth. Do you know what he did? First he turned green, then he turned black and then he turned bright pink, and a bunch of flowers grew out of the top of his head.

'Why! You're not a frightening monster at all!' cried Molly.

'Aren't I?' said the Monster.

'No!' said Molly, and a beautiful ribbon tied in a bow suddenly appeared right round the Monster's middle. And Molly took hold of the ribbon and pulled it and the Monster opened up and inside was a little rabbit who looked very frightened and said: 'Oh please! Don't put me in a pie!'

And Brave Molly said: 'I won't put you in a pie this time, but don't go around trying to frighten little children in future.'

'No . . . I promise,' said the rabbit, and scuttled off out of the hut.

And just then the sky cleared and the sun came out, and Brave Molly set off home again, and she didn't meet another monster all the rest of the way.

The Sea Tiger

HERE WAS ONCE A TIGER who told the most enormous lies. No matter how hard he tried, he just couldn't tell the truth.

Once the monkey asked the tiger where he was going. The tiger replied that he was on his way to the moon, where he kept a store of tiger-cheese which made his eyes brighter than the sun so that he could see in the dark. But in fact he was going behind a bush for a snooze.

Another time, the snake asked the tiger round for lunch, but the tiger said that he couldn't come because a man had heard him singing in the jungle, and had asked him to go to the big city that very afternoon to sing in the opera.

'Oh!' said the snake. 'Before you go, won't you sing something for me?'

'Ah no,' said the tiger. 'If I sing before I've had my breakfast, my tail swells up and turns into a sausage, and I get followed around by sausage-flies all day.'

One day, all the animals in the jungle held a meeting, and decided they'd cure the tiger of telling such enormous lies. So they sent the monkey off to find the wizard who lived in the snow-capped mountains. The monkey climbed for seven days and seven nights, and he got higher and higher until at last he reached the cave in the snow where the wizard lived.

At the entrance to the cave he called out: 'Old wizard, are you there?'

And a voice called out: 'Come in, monkey, I've been expecting you.'

So the monkey went into the cave. He found the wizard busy preparing spells, and he told him that the animals of the jungle wanted to cure the tiger of telling such enormous lies.

'Very well,' said the wizard. 'Take this potion, and pour it into the tiger's ears when he is asleep.'

'But what will it do, wizard?' asked the monkey.

The wizard smiled and said: 'Rest assured, once you've given him this potion, everything the tiger says will be true all right.'

So the monkey took the potion and went back to the jungle where he told the other animals what they had to do.

That day, while the tiger was having his usual nap behind the bush, all the other animals gathered round in a circle and the monkey crept up very cautiously to the tiger and carefully poured a little of the potion into first one of the tiger's ears and then into the other. Then he ran back to the other animals, and they all called out: 'Tiger! Tiger! Wake up, tiger!'

After a while, the tiger opened one eye, and then the other. He was a bit surprised to find all the other animals of the jungle standing around him in a circle.

'Have you been asleep?' asked the lion.

'Oh no,' said the tiger, 'I was just lying here, planning my next expedition to the bottom of the ocean.'

When they heard this, all the other animals shook their heads and said: 'The wizard's potion hasn't worked. Tiger's still telling as whopping lies as ever!'

But just then the tiger found himself leaping to his feet and bounding across the jungle. 'But it's true!' he cried to his own surprise.

'What are you doing, tiger?' they asked.

'I'm going to fly there!' he called and, sure enough, he spread out his legs and soared up high above the trees and across the top of the jungle.

Now if there's one thing tigers don't like, it's heights, and so the tiger yelled out: 'Help! I *am* flying! Get me down!'

But he found himself flying on and on until the jungle was far behind him and he flew over the snow-capped mountains where the wizard lived. The wizard looked up at the tiger flying overhead and smiled to himself and said: 'Ha-ha, old tiger, you'll always tell the truth now. For anything you say will become true – even if it wasn't before!'

And the tiger flew on and on, and he got colder and colder and, if there's one thing tigers hate worse than heights, it's being cold.

At length he found himself flying out over the sea, and then suddenly he dropped like a stone, until he came down splash in the middle of the ocean. Now if there's one thing that tigers hate more than heights and cold, it's getting wet.

'Urrrrgh!' said the tiger, but down and down he sank, right to the bottom of the ocean, and all the fish came up to him and stared, so he chased them off with his tail.

Then he looked up and he could see the bottom of the waves high above him, and he swam up and up, and just as he was running out of breath he reached the surface. Then he struggled and splashed and tried to swim for the shore.

Just then a fishing-boat came by, and all the fishermen gasped in amazement to see a tiger swimming in the middle of the ocean. Then one of them laughed and pointed at the tiger and said: 'Look! A sea tiger!'

And they all laughed and pointed at the tiger, and, if there's one thing tigers hate worse than heights and cold and getting wet, it's being laughed at.

The poor tiger paddled away as fast as he could, but it was a long way to the shore, and eventually the fishermen threw one of their nets over him and hauled him on to the boat.

'Oh ho!' they laughed. 'Now we can make a fortune by getting this sea tiger to perform tricks in the circus!'

Now this made the tiger really angry because, if there's one thing tigers hate more than heights and cold and getting wet and being laughed at, it's performing tricks in the circus. So as soon as they landed he tore up the net, and leapt out of the boat, and ran home to the forest as fast as his legs would carry him.

And he never told any lies, *ever* again.

The Wind Ghosts

WHEN THE WIND IS HOWLING ROUND THE HOUSE and tearing at the clouds, our ears are filled with noise. Chimney pots rattle, doors bang, windows shake. But in between the blasts, when the wind is still for a moment, you can sometimes hear, very faintly, the pitter-patter footsteps of the ghosts who follow the wind. Here is the story of one such ghost.

Once there were two friends who set off to seek their fortunes. On the first day, they came to a wide river, and did not know how to get across. So they walked along the river bank until they came to a little tumbledown hut, where an old woman was sitting making a necklace of bones.

'How do we get across this river, old woman?' they asked.

The old woman kept on threading the bones on the string as if they were beads, and said: 'There are two ways to cross the river. One is free, and one will cost you.'

'How can that be?' asked the two friends.

'Well,' said the old woman, 'one way is to swim across. That's free. The other way is to take the boat that leaves from here at midnight, but that will cost you, for once you step on board you must give the boatmen whatever he asks for.'

'I don't want to get wet,' said the first friend, whose name was Jonathan. 'I'll take the boat.'

'Who knows what the boatman might ask for!' said David. 'I'll swim.'

So the two friends agreed to meet the next day on the other side. Then David tied all his belongings in his shirt, and put them on his head, and swam across. It was a wide river, and the current took him a long way downstream, but eventually he got to the other side. There he lit a fire and waited until his friend Jonathan arrived.

'Well?' asked David. 'What did the boatman ask for?'

'Oh . . . he wanted the moon,' said Jonathan.

'So what did you give him?' asked David.

'Oh . . . I just got out my cup and dipped it in the river and handed it to him so that, when he looked into it, there was the moon, shining up at him.'

Well, the two friends went on their way, and on the second day they came to a deep chasm. There they found a little old man, sitting outside a cave.

'How do we get across this chasm?' they asked.

'There are two ways,' said the little old man. 'One way will take a minute, the other way will take a month.'

'How can that be?' they asked.

'Well, one way is to walk all round the edge of the chasm, and that will take you a month,' said the little old man. 'The other way is to ask the eagle that lives on this mountain to give you a ride on his back. But if he does, you must answer any question he asks you as you fly over, otherwise he will drop you into the chasm.'

'I'm not going to risk that!' said David. 'I'll walk round the edge, even if it takes a month.'

'I can answer any question,' said Jonathan. 'I'll fly on the eagle's back.'

So the two friends agreed to meet in a month's time. David walked and walked for a whole month, and eventually he reached the spot on the other side of the chasm where they had agreed to meet, and there – sure enough – was his friend Jonathan waiting for him.

'What was the eagle's question?' asked David.

'Oh . . . he wanted to know where he could always find the summer sun in midwinter,' replied Jonathan.

'What did you tell him?' asked David.

'Oh . . . I told him to find one blade of grass, for you must know that all plants store the summer sun in their leaves.'

So the two friends went on their way until they came to the shore of a sea. There they found an old sailor, so they asked him how they could cross the sea.

'There are two ways,' said the old sailor. 'One way is dangerous, the other way is safe.'

'How can that be?' they asked.

'One way is to sail across on a boat. That will be full of danger, for the sea is deep and there are storms and high waves and sea-monsters. The other way is to go to the wizard of the sea, and ask him to get you across by his magic. That is quite

safe, but with this warning: you will have to do whatever the wizard of the sea wants first, or else you will never get across at all.'

'I will sail across,' said David, 'for I would rather face the dangers of the sea than put myself in the wizard's hands.'

'I can do whatever the wizard asks me to,' said Jonathan. 'I'll go by magic.'

So Jonathan went to the wizard and swore to do whatever the wizard asked of him.

'There's only one thing you need do for me,' said the wizard, 'and that's not so difficult for someone who can give the moon away and who knows where to find the summer sun in midwinter.'

'What is it I must do?' asked Jonathan.

'You must catch the wind,' said the wizard. And just then a breeze blew across the shore, and Jonathan set off after it.

Meanwhile David had built himself a boat. He spread his sail, and the wind blew him across the ocean. Sometimes the wind blew up a storm, and sometimes it blew him the wrong way, and he fought with the rain and the cold and the sea-monsters, but at length he got to the other side. There he built a windmill, and the wind turned the sails of the mill, and he became a miller. He never grew rich, but he was never poor, and – for all I know – he was happy enough.

Jonathan, however, never *was* able to catch the wind, and to this day he chases after it, and in between the blasts of a storm you may hear the pitter-patter of his footsteps. He cannot stop and he cannot catch it, for he is now a wind ghost. And yet – for all I know – he *too* is happy enough . . . in his way.

The Big Noses

THERE WAS ONCE AN ISLAND in the middle of the ocean, where everybody's nose was far too big. The chief of the island got in a boat, and sailed to the place where the wisest of all men lived.

'Now, what is the problem?' asked the wisest of all men.

'Well,' said the chief of the island, 'all my people are unhappy because their noses are too big. We can't get our sweaters over our heads because our noses are so big. We can't enjoy a drink without hitting our noses on the other side of the cup. We can't kiss each other, because our noses get in the way. But worst of all, we don't even like each other, because of our ugly great noses. Can you help us by making our noses smaller?'

'Well,' said the wisest of all men, 'I cannot make your noses smaller. Only the magician who lives by the burning lake could do that – and even he could not do it for *all* your people. But come back in three days' time, and perhaps I shall be able to help you.'

So the chief of the island stayed in that land for two days and two nights. And while he was there, he went to the magician who lived by the burning lake and the magician cast a spell over his nose and made it very small indeed. And on the third day, the chief went back to the wisest of all men, and said: 'Well, have you thought of an answer?'

The wisest of all men looked at the island chief in amazement. Finally he said: 'Is that really *you*?'

And the chief said: 'Yes, of course it is.'

And the wisest of all men said: 'But what has happened to your nose?' So the chief of the island told him how he had been to the magician. And the wisest of all men shook his grey head, and said: 'You seek one solution for yourself and another for your people, and that's not good.'

'Well, it's too late now,' replied the chief, 'so what is your solution for my people?'

'First,' said the wisest of all men, 'you must go to the volcano that lies on the other side of this land, and take the ashes from its mouth, and rub them into your hair and hands and all over your body. Then put on these robes, and return to your people and tell them that you are Chan Tanda.'

The chief looked amazed, and said: 'But *you* are Chan Tanda, the wisest of all men. Why should I pretend to be you?'

'You must,' said Chan Tanda, 'and, believe me, you will thank me for it.'

So the chief took the clothes and Chan Tanda told him what he was to say to his people, and then he went to the volcano, and climbed to the very top, where the smoke and flames came billowing out of the ground. And he rubbed the ashes into his hair and hands and all over his body until he was a dusty grey colour, just like Chan Tanda himself. And he put on the clothes and sailed back to his people.

When he arrived, they all said: 'Where is our chief?'

And he replied, as he had been instructed: 'Your chief says he will not come back to this island until his people have become more reasonable.'

'What does he mean?' they all cried. 'We may have big noses, but we're not fools! Tell him to come back!'

'He says he won't come back until you've changed some of your foolish ways,' said the chief of the island.

'What foolish ways?' they said. 'What does he mean?'

'For a start, he says you must stop sitting out in the rain playing ludo.'

'But we like sitting out in the rain playing ludo!' they cried.

'Secondly, you must stop using egg-cups for your tea.'

'But we like drinking tea out of egg-cups!' they cried.

'And thirdly, you must bend your heads to one side when you kiss.'

'But we've always kept them upright!' they cried.

'Otherwise your chief will never return,' said the chief of the island.

Well, they held a meeting, and decided to do what was asked so that their leader would return. And before long they discovered that when they didn't sit out in the rain playing ludo, their sweaters didn't shrink, and they were able to put them on over their heads without their noses getting in the way. And when they gave up

drinking tea out of egg-cups, they found that their noses no longer hit the other side. And when they bent their heads to one side, they could kiss just fine. Before long, they even started to like each other, and soon they were all living happily enough, and realized that there never had been anything wrong with their noses in the first place.

But the chief of the island had to return to the wisest of all men, and get him to persuade the magician who lived by the burning lake to change *his* nose back to its proper size again, before he dared to go home to his own people.

A Fish of the World

 HERRING ONCE DECIDED TO SWIM right round the world. 'I'm tired of the North Sea,' he said. 'I want to find out what else there is in the world.'

So he swam off south into the deep Atlantic. He swam and he swam far far away from the seas he knew, through the warm waters of the equator and on down into the South Atlantic. And all the time he saw many strange and wonderful fish that he had never seen before. Once he was nearly eaten by a shark, and once he was nearly electrocuted by an electric eel, and once he was nearly stung by a sting-ray. But he swam on and on, round the tip of Africa and into the Indian Ocean. And he passed by devilfish and sailfish and sawfish and swordfish and bluefish and blackfish and mudfish and sunfish, and he was amazed by the different shapes and sizes and colours.

On he swam, into the Java Sea, and he saw fish that leapt out of the water and fish that lived on the bottom of the sea and fish that could walk on their fins. And on he swam, through the Coral Sea, where the shells of millions and millions of tiny creatures had turned to rock and stood as big as mountains. But still he swam on, into the wide Pacific. He swam over the deepest parts of the ocean, where the water is so deep that it is inky black at the bottom, and the fish carry lanterns over their heads, and some have lights on their tails. And through the Pacific he swam, and then he turned north and headed up to the cold Siberian Sea, where huge white icebergs sailed past him like mighty ships. And still he swam on and on and into the frozen Arctic Ocean, where the sea is forever covered in ice. And on he went, past Greenland and Iceland, and finally he swam home into his own North Sea.

All his friends and relations gathered round and made a great fuss of him. They had a big feast and offered him the very best food they could find. But the herring just yawned and said: 'I've swum round the entire world. I have seen everything there is to see, and I have eaten more exotic and wonderful dishes than you could

possibly imagine.' And he refused to eat anything.

Then his friends and relations begged him to come home and live with them, but he refused. 'I've been everwhere there is, and that old rock is too dull and small for me.' And he went off and lived on his own.

And when the breeding season came, he refused to join in the spawning, saying: 'I've swum around the entire world, and now I know how many fish there are in the world, I can't be interested in herrings anymore.'

Eventually, one of the oldest of the herrings swam up to him, and said: 'Listen. If you don't spawn with us, some herrings' eggs will go unfertilized and will not turn into healthy young herring. If you don't live with your family, you'll make them sad. And if you don't eat, you'll die.'

But the herring said: 'I don't mind. I've been everywhere there is to go, I've seen everything there is to see, and now I know everything there is to know.'

The old fish shook his head. 'No-one has ever seen everything there is to see,' he said, 'nor known everything there is to know.'

'Look,' said the herring, 'I've swum through the North Sea, the Atlantic Ocean, the Indian Ocean, the Java Sea, the Coral Sea, the great Pacific Ocean, the Siberian Sea and the frozen Arctic. Tell me, what else is there for me to see or know?'

'I don't know,' said the old herring, 'but there may be something.'

Well, just then, a fishing-boat came by, and all the herrings were caught in a net and taken to market that very day. And a man bought the herring, and ate it for his supper.

And he never knew that it had swum right round the world, and had seen everything there was to see, and knew everything there was to know.

Tim O'Leary

UNDREDS OF YEARS AGO a goblin sat on the bank of a river, dipping his toes in the water. Towards the end of the day, a farmer came walking home from his fields. When he saw the little goblin he rubbed his eyes and looked again.

'What sort of thing are you?' he asked.

'I'm Tim O'Leary,' said the goblin.

'How can that be?' said the farmer. 'Tim O'Leary's my best friend, and he don't look a bit like you.'

'Ah!' sighed the goblin. 'I found a cave that was full of witch's treasure, and I would have carried it all off, but I cut my feet on some magic rocks, and turned into a goblin as you can see.'

'But what are you doing with your feet in the river?' asked the farmer.

'I'm trying to wash the magic off my feet,' replied the goblin, 'but it's no good.'

'Oh deary me, Tim,' said the farmer, 'whatever can we do?'

'The only way to turn me back into Tim O'Leary is to steal the witch's treasure and throw every single bit of it into the deepest ocean.'

'I'll do that!' cried the farmer.

'But mind you don't cut your feet on the magic rocks!' said the goblin.

'I won't,' said the farmer, 'I have on my toughest boots.' And he set off to find the cave.

It was almost night when he found it, so he lit a torch and ventured in. First he came to a long tunnel, where the floor and the walls and the ceiling were all of sharp rocks. So he walked very slowly and very carefully along the tunnel, and he managed to get to the other end of it without cutting himself.

There he found three great doors. One was made of wood. One was made of iron. And one was made of stone. Just as he was wondering which one to try, he heard a croak behind him. He turned round and found a frog sitting on a rock.

'You want to know what lies behind the doors?' asked the frog.

'Yes,' said the farmer.

'Very well, I'll tell you, if you promise to give me a jewel from the witch's treasure.'

'I can't do that,' replied the farmer, 'I have to throw every single bit of the witch's treasure into the ocean, so that the goblin can turn back into Tim O'Leary.'

'Huh!' said the frog. 'Don't believe that goblin. He's no more Tim O'Leary than I am. He just wants to get his hands on the witch's treasure.'

'Well, why doesn't he come and get it himself?' asked the farmer.

'He's a water-goblin,' said the frog. 'Very powerful, you know, but he must keep touching water. That's why he sits with his toes in the river.'

Well, the farmer didn't know who to believe, but he said to himself: 'I set out to save Tim O'Leary, and that's what I'll do.'

'Come,' said the frog, 'you can give me a jewel from the witch's treasure and then keep the rest for yourself.'

'No,' replied the farmer, 'I must save Tim O'Leary.'

'You fool!' screamed the frog, shaking with anger. Then he grew larger and larger, and turned brown and then black and suddenly there was a little old elf.

'You fool!' he screamed. 'You'll never get the witch's treasure now! It lies behind one of the doors, but behind another lies a monster that will tear you to pieces, and behind the third lies a hole that will suck you in. Now you won't know which is which and I shan't tell you!' And he disappeared in a puff of smoke that smelt curiously of nettle beer.

Well, the farmer was very frightened, but he was determined to help Tim O'Leary. So he covered himself from head to foot in mud and got a long pole that stretched the length of the three great doors. Then he opened the first door that was made of wood. Immediately there was a whooshing noise and he saw a terrible black hole, and he felt himself being sucked towards it. And suddenly stones and rocks from the cave were flying past him, and all disappearing into that terrible black hole. But the farmer clung tight to his pole, and because it was wider than the doorway it couldn't go through. So the farmer struggled and strained and eventually he managed to shut the door with a great bang, and the sucking wind died down and the cave grew still again.

'Phew!' said the farmer. 'Now which of the next two doors has the treasure, and which has the monster that will tear me to pieces?'

Finally he decided to try the iron door. He opened it very, very cautiously,

expecting a terrible monster to leap out at him at any moment. But all was quiet. He looked in and found himself gazing into a high hall, lit by candles, and in the centre of the hall was a great iron chest, with a golden lock.

The farmer looked around the hall and there on the wall hung a great golden key. So he took the key and eagerly opened up the treasure chest. Whereupon there was a terrible roar and out jumped a hideous monster with great claws and bulging eyes. And it stretched out its claws to seize the farmer, but, because he was all covered in mud, he slipped through them, and ran as hard as he could for the door. He got there in the nick of time and slammed it shut just as the monster sprang again, so that it crashed against the great door and the iron rang and the monster roared.

Then the farmer opened the last of the three doors, that was made of stone. And there lay the witch's treasure. The poor man had never seen so many precious stones and so much gold and silver.

'It would be a crime', he said to himself, 'to throw all that into the ocean but, if that's the only way to save Tim O'Leary, that's what I must do.'

So he put it all into a great sack and carried it down to the river and put it into a boat and set off for the sea.

Well, he hadn't gone very far before he heard singing coming from the back of the boat, and there he found the goblin sitting trailing a toe in the water. In this way, they sailed out into the wide open ocean, until the goblin suddenly said: 'Here we are!'

And the farmer picked up the sack of treasure, and he took one last look at it and said: 'I shall never see such wealth again. But if this is the only way to turn you back into Tim O'Leary, away it goes!' And he emptied all the precious jewels and silver and gold into the sea.

'Ah ha!' cried the goblin. 'Thank you very much! I was never Tim O'Leary and he was never me!' And with that he jumped into the waves and disappeared with the treasure.

Well, the farmer went home, and he found Tim O'Leary sitting on a wall.

'Oh,' said the farmer, 'because of you, I've lost the richest treasure I've ever seen,' and he told him the whole story. And Tim O'Leary put his arm round the farmer and said: 'Leave the treasure to the goblins. You've proved yourself a true friend to me and a true friend I'll be to you, and that's worth more than all the gold and silver and precious jewels in the world.'

The Witch and the Rainbow Cat

SMALL GIRL WAS WALKING along the banks of a river on a hot summer's day when, quite by chance, she came across a little house. It had a front door and windows and a chimney and a little garden that ran down to the river, but it was very, very small. The girl could touch the roof if she reached up, and she had to bend her head to look in at the windows.

'I wonder if anyone's at home?' she said to herself. So she knocked on the door and waited, but there was no answer. So she tried the door and it opened easily.

'Hello?' she called. 'Is there anyone at home?' But there was no answer. Now the little girl knew that she shouldn't go into a strange house without being invited, but it was all so curious and so small that she just *had* to look inside. So she bent her head, and stepped into the house.

Everything in the house was perfect, but half the size of normal things. She didn't have to stand on tip-toe to look on to the tables. She didn't have to stand on a chair to reach the kitchen sink or look out of the windows, and the door handles were all just the right height. There was a sitting-room with a fireplace and a mirror over the mantelpiece, and she could see into the mirror perfectly well, just like her mother could at home, without having to climb on anything. But she noticed one very curious thing: the reflection of herself that she saw in the mirror was quite grown-up.

At first she thought it was a trick of the light, and she looked around the room at the other things, but when she turned back to the mirror, sure enough – instead of a little girl, there was a fully grown-up woman looking back at her. She blinked and stared again. It was definitely *her* reflection: the dress it was wearing was exactly

the same as the dress she was wearing, and when she touched her nose the reflection touched *its* nose, and when she touched her ear, the reflection touched *its* ear ... and suddenly she realized – she was looking at herself as a grown-up woman.

How long she stood there, staring into that mirror, I don't know, but suddenly she heard the latch on the front door open, and she heard some footsteps coming slowly into the house ... tip ... tap ... tip ... tap ... and all at once she remembered that she shouldn't be there, so she quickly hid herself behind a little cupboard, feeling very frightened.

She heard the footsteps go into the kitchen ... tip ... tap ... tip ... tap ... and then go out of the kitchen and slowly start to come towards the sitting-room ... tip ... tap ... tip ... tap. Nearer and nearer they came and the little girl's heart beat faster and faster, until suddenly the footsteps stopped and turned and went upstairs. The little girl took her chance and ran for the front door, but it was locked. She ran to the back door, but that too was locked, and there was no key. She tried the windows but they were all tight shut, and she couldn't open any of them. And so she ran back and hid behind the cupboard in the sitting-room.

Well, she crouched there for quite a long time, wondering what on earth she was going to do, when she heard the footsteps coming downstairs again ... tip ... tap ... tip ... tap. This time they turned towards the sitting-room and kept on coming, closer and closer, until they walked right in. The little girl peered out from behind the cupboard, and do you know what she saw? She saw a little old witch in a green hat and a green cloak, and on her shoulder was a cat that was all the colours of the rainbow.

The little girl didn't know what to do, so she just kept quiet. And the little old witch stopped and looked about her, and said: 'Who's been looking in my mirror? I can see a child there!'

The poor girl trembled with fright and kept just as quiet as she could, but she heard the little old witch coming towards the cupboard, and suddenly there she was, looking down at her with piercing green eyes.

'Who are you?' asked the old witch. 'What are you doing in my house?'

'Please,' said the little girl, 'my name is Rose and I didn't mean any harm.'

'*Didn't* mean any harm?' screamed the old witch. 'Didn't mean any *harm*! You've looked in my mirror!'

'Please,' said Rose, 'shouldn't I have done?'

'Of course you shouldn't have!' screamed the witch. 'Now I'll have to keep you here for ever!'

'Oh please, let me go home,' cried Rose, 'and I'll never come and bother you again.'

'No! You've looked in my mirror!' cried the witch. 'You can't go back now! You'll stay here and be my servant!'

Well, poor Rose wept and pleaded with the little green witch, but there was nothing she could do. The witch took her up to the attic at the top of the little house and locked her in. The attic had no windows and was bare and dark and full of cobwebs. Poor Rose sat down on the dusty floor and cried, for she didn't know what she was going to do.

Suddenly she felt something soft brushing up against her, and she nearly jumped out of her skin. But when she looked down she found it was just the rainbow-coloured cat, rubbing itself up against her legs.

'Hello,' said the rainbow cat. 'You can ask me three questions.'

Rose was so astonished to hear the cat talk that, without stopping to think, she exclaimed: 'But how is it you can talk?'

The rainbow cat yawned and replied: 'I would have thought that was obvious – the witch put a spell on me. Two questions left. If I were you, I'd think more carefully about the next.'

Rose thought carefully about the next question, and then asked: 'Why doesn't the witch like me looking in her mirror?'

'A better question,' replied the cat, stretching itself. 'She doesn't like you looking in the mirror because she is the Witch of the Future, and in that mirror she sees the things that are to come. She is the only person that can know those things, and once you know them she'll never let you go. One question left.'

Rose thought very carefully about what was the best question to ask the rainbow cat next, but try as she might she could not decide. She thought: 'If I ask him how to escape from here, that wouldn't stop the old witch catching me again. If I ask him how I can get home, that wouldn't stop the old witch from finding me there. . . .'

At length the rainbow cat asked: 'Well? Have you thought of your last question?'

'Not yet,' replied Rose.

'Very well,' said the cat, 'I'll wait.'

Just then the door flew open and in burst the witch. She thrust a bundle of old clothes towards Rose and said: 'Here is a servant's uniform. You must put it on, or I'll turn you into a mad dog.'

Poor Rose trembled with fright, but she took off her own clothes and put the uniform on. It was grey and drab, and it made her feel miserable.

'Now,' said the witch, 'you must start to work for me.' And she made poor Rose scrub the floors from morning till evening, all that day and all the next day. And when Rose begged to be allowed to do some other work, the Witch of the Future shook her head and said: 'No! You must keep your eyes on the floor so that you don't go looking in my mirror again.'

Poor Rose had to scrub the witch's floors day in, day out, and at night she was so exhausted that she would go to bed without once raising her eyes from the floor. Day after day, week after week, the witch kept her at it, until poor Rose's back was bent and her hands were sore, and she never raised her eyes from the floor ever. And she worked so hard that she forgot about everything else until, one day, when the witch was out in the forest collecting toads, Rose suddenly felt the rainbow cat rubbing itself up against her leg.

'Rainbow cat! I'd forgotten about you!' she cried.

'Well,' said the cat, 'have you thought of your last question yet?'

Rose stopped her scrubbing for a moment, and then said: 'I'll ask you my last question tomorrow.'

'Very well,' said the cat, 'I'll wait.'

All that night, although she was exhausted from her scrubbing, Rose couldn't sleep. She was too busy trying to work out the best question to ask the rainbow cat, but she still couldn't decide.

The next morning she could hardly get up to scrub the floors, and she kept yawning and feeling faint.

'Now then!' screamed the Witch of the Future. 'What are you doing? Get on with your scrubbing, girl, or I'll turn you into a cabbage and make you into cabbage soup!'

Then the witch went out to the forest to catch some bats. Rose was scrubbing the doorstep, watching the witch go, when she noticed a small bird in the garden, with its leg caught in one of the witch's traps. Although Rose knew that the witch would be very angry, she couldn't bear to see the bird in such pain, and so she put down her scrubbing brush and went and released it, and then went back to her scrubbing.

The next moment, she felt something rub against her leg and there was the rainbow cat again.

'Well,' said the rainbow cat, 'have you thought of your last question?'

'Not quite,' said Rose.

'I can't wait any longer,' replied the rainbow cat.

Just then, the bird flew down and landed on Rose's shoulder, and said: 'I can tell you what to ask.' And it whispered in Rose's ear, and then flew off again.

'Well,' said the rainbow cat, 'what is your question?'

Rose looked at the cat and took a deep breath and then said as the bird had told her: 'Tell me, rainbow cat, why can't I choose my own future?'

At these words, the rainbow cat looked up and smiled, and his colours all started changing and glowing and spinning round and round. 'But you can!' he cried. 'The Witch of the Future has no power without her mirror – break that and you are free.'

Just then, Rose looked up and saw the witch coming out of the wood towards her. Without another word, Rose turned and ran back into the little house, and took the mirror off the wall and hurled it to the ground so that it smashed into smithereens. Everything went still. Then there was a dreadful scream, and there glaring at her in the doorway stood the Witch of the Future, only she looked a thousand years older. Rose summoned up all her courage but, before she could speak, the witch stumbled and fell to the floor. At that moment Rose heard a creak, and saw the wall of the house start to crumble. So she ran, and she didn't stop running until she reached the gate at the bottom of the garden. There she turned, in time to see the little house collapse in a cloud of dust, and an ordinary black cat walked out and rubbed up against her legs.

'Is that you, rainbow cat?' asked Rose. But the cat didn't reply. It simply strolled off into the wood. And Rose changed back into her own clothes, and ran home as fast as she possibly could.

The Monster Tree

THERE WAS ONCE A TREE THAT GREW in a wood not far from here. It was a very special tree. Its leaves were red and its trunk was green and on it grew apples that were bright blue. And nobody ever ate the bright blue apples that hung from the tree, because they knew that if they did they would meet a monster before the day was out.

One day a boy was walking with his mother in the wood, and they passed the Monster Tree. 'Oh, can I have one of those bright blue apples?' said the boy.

'No,' said his mother, 'you know you mustn't, because anyone who eats one will meet a monster before the day is out.'

The little boy didn't say anything, but he thought to himself: 'Piffle!' and he resolved there and then that he would try one of those bright blue apples for himself.

So that night, when his mother and father were safely tucked up in bed, he took his satchel and stole out of the house and down the garden and through the village. The moon made everything blue and silver, and the houses looked dark and sinister, and he began to feel a little bit frightened at being all on his own.

Soon he came to the end of the village, and he looked along the lonely path that led to the wood where the Monster Tree grew, and he felt even more frightened. 'But I don't believe in monsters,' he said to himself, and he set off along the path.

Before long he came to the edge of a wood. The trees stretched up high above him, and the wood was dark and full of strange noises, and he didn't like it at all.

83

But he said to himself: 'I'm not scared of monsters.' Then he summoned up all his courage, and stepped into the dark wood.

Well, he hadn't gone very far before he heard a hideous noise, and he saw a horrible pair of yellow eyes peering out at him from the darkness, and a terrible voice said: 'You'll make a tasty meal for the monsters in the wood.'

He was so frightened that his knees knocked together, but he kept on walking. And he hadn't gone much farther when there was an awful screech, and something flew out of a tree and pulled his hair and screamed: 'The monsters are hungry tonight! The monsters are hungry tonight!'

Now he was so scared that his teeth started chattering, but he kept on walking towards the Monster Tree.

And just as he was passing an old hollow oak, a terrible creature leapt out in front of him, with great long nails and burning eyes and fire coming out of its ears and it screamed: 'They'll break your bones! They'll drink your blood! Go back at once!'

And the boy was so frightened that his hair stood on end, and he nearly turned right round and ran home to his bed. But he didn't. And the creature gave a terrible shriek and rushed at him. The boy jumped up and grabbed a branch, and then leapt over the creature's head, and ran as fast as he could until he reached the Monster Tree. He pulled off as many of the bright blue apples as he could carry in his satchel, and ran home as fast as his legs could take him. And when he got home, he jumped into bed, hid under the blankets and ate one of the bright blue apples from the Monster Tree all alone in the dark, and then he fell asleep.

In his dreams that night he met more monsters than you could ever imagine in a whole year. And when he woke up the next morning, he told his mother all about the Monster Tree and his terrible journey in the night. His mother was very cross, and she took his satchel and opened it up to throw those apples from the Monster Tree on the fire. But when she looked into the satchel she couldn't see any bright blue apples – they were just ordinary apples. And that morning, the villagers went into the wood to cut that Monster Tree down, but do you know what? They couldn't find it. And to this day it has never been seen again.

The Snuff-Box

HERE WAS ONCE A DARK CASTLE that stood on the edge of a black and bottomless lake. People said that once the castle had been full of light and laughter, but now it stood empty because no–one dared live in it, for they said that something horrible lay in the black lake.

One day, however, a wicked witch came to the dark castle, and gazed down into the dark, deep waters of the bottomless lake. She picked up a toad that was sitting on the bank, and put a spell on it.

'Now then toad,' she said, 'I want you to swim down to the bottom of the lake, and bring me what you find there.'

So the toad disappeared under the water, and was gone for a whole day. At length, however, its head bobbed up to the surface again, and it said: 'Witch! I swam down, and I swam down, deeper and deeper, where there is no sound, and there is no light, but I could not find any bottom to the lake.'

'There must be a bottom, toad!' cried the witch. 'Try again!'

This time the toad disappeared into the dark, deep waters, and was gone for two whole days. When it came up to the surface again it said: 'Witch! I swam down and I swam down, deeper and deeper, where there is no sound and no light, and at last I did indeed reach the bottom, but I could not see anything, and I could not stay there, for it is as black and cold as the grave.'

The witch cried: 'You lazy toad! Here is a lantern – go down and look again!'

So the toad took the lantern, and disappeared into the dismal waters once more. This time it was gone for three whole days. And twilight fell on the fourth, and still the old witch sat waiting by the black lake. At last the toad reappeared, and said: 'Witch! I swam down, and I swam down, deeper and deeper, where there is no sound and there is no light, and at last I reached the bottom where it is as black and cold as the grave, and no bird has ever sung. I searched that foul floor by the dim light of this lantern, and at last I found this. . . .' And it opened its hand, and there lay a small snuff-box.

'Give it to me at once!' cried the witch.

But the toad held on to it, and said: 'What is my reward?'

'Give me the snuff-box,' replied the witch, 'and I will turn you into a prince!'

'Very well,' said the toad, and it gave the witch the snuff-box.

The moment it did so, the witch burst into a cackle of evil laughter. 'Impertinent creature!' she cried. 'You think I'd turn you into a prince, do you? Very well! I will!' And with that she waved her hands, and the toad did indeed turn into a prince, but into the ugliest, hunch-backed prince you ever could imagine, with one leg shorter than the other and warts on his face.

'Ah-ha!' cried the witch. 'Enjoy your reward!' And she vanished into the dark castle, clutching the snuff-box.

Now the wicked witch knew that in the snuff-box, many, many years ago, a demon had been imprisoned, who had once brought terror on all the people of that land. So she held it tight, and whispered: 'Demon in the box, are you there?'

And a tiny voice said: 'Oh! Yes. Please open the box. I've been in here *so* long. . . .'

But the witch held on to it all the tighter, and said: 'If I release you, you must promise to be my slave and do as I command you for one whole year and a day, so that I become rich and rule all this land. Then you will be free to go where you will.'

'Indeed I shall!' cried the small voice. So the witch opened the snuff-box, and immediately there was a terrifying roar, and a blast of scalding air threw the witch back against the wall, and smoke poured into the room, as out leapt the demon with a terrible cry: 'At last!'

'Don't forget you are my slave for one whole year and a day!' cried the witch.

'I am nobody's slave!' cried the demon, and he touched the witch on the nape of the neck, and she turned into a millstone, and he cast her into the cold, black lake.

Meanwhile, the toad-prince had clambered in at the window of the dark castle, and he had seen all that had happened between the witch and demon of the snuff-box. And he said to himself: 'I fetched this demon up from the bottom of the bottomless lake. I must send him back there.' So he jumped down into the great hall.

'Who dares to enter my castle?' roared the demon.

'Demon!' said the toad-prince. 'Are you going to rob the people of this land?'

'Indeed I am!' roared the demon.

'Are you going to kill their dogs and steal their children?' asked the toad-prince.

'Indeed I am!' cried the demon.

'And will you make them poor and live in terror of you?'

'Indeed I shall!' bellowed the demon.

'Then let me help you!' said the toad-prince. 'For, as you see, I am ugly and unwanted, and I should like to do all the harm I can.'

'Very good!' cried the demon.

'But first,' said the toad-prince, 'I must know how powerful you really are.'

'I can easily show you,' said the demon, and he waved his hand, and a ball of fire appeared in mid-air. It circled round them once, and then flew out of the window.

'Hmmm,' said the toad-prince. 'Can't you do anything else?'

'Come with me,' said the demon, and he took the toad-prince on to the roof of the castle. 'Watch this,' he said, and spread his wings, and flew up into the air so high that he tore a hole in the sky, and a strange light shone down upon the earth.

Then the demon plucked up a pine tree, threaded a trailing vine through its roots, and sewed the sky up again.

'Well,' said the toad-prince, 'that's not bad, but it's still not what I would call *really* powerful.'

'And what would *that* be?' roared the demon who was, perhaps justly, rather piqued.

The toad-prince bent down, and picked up a speck of dust, and said: 'Now if a creature as big and powerful as you could get inside that grain of dust – *that's* what I'd call *really* powerful!'

'Child's play!' exclaimed the demon, and made himself smaller and smaller, until he was no bigger than a speck of dust. Whereupon, before he could change back again, the prince picked him up and put him back in the snuff-box, and fastened the lid tight. Then he threw the snuff-box back into the black lake.

After that, the toad-prince lived in the castle, and ruled the land about with kindness and justice. And, although he was hunch-backed, the people of that land loved him, and laughter and light returned to the dark castle once again.

The Man Who Owned The Earth

**A** POOR MAN ONCE WENT to a wizard and said: 'Make me the richest man in the world.'

So the wizard gave him a ball of clay and three potions, and said: 'You must use these very carefully, for they are very strong magic. The first is very powerful, for if you were to pour it all on to the ball of magic clay, all the gold in the world would be yours. The second is even more powerful, for if you were to pour all *that* on the ball of clay, all the silver in the world would be yours. But the third is the most powerful of all, for if you poured *that* on to the clay, all the wood in the world would be yours.'

The man was very pleased, and said: 'If I had all the gold there is, I wouldn't need wood or silver! I would own the earth!'

'Indeed you would,' replied the wizard. 'But that must never be. One drop of each potion will make you rich beyond your wildest dreams. The rest you must bring back to me or you will end your days as poor as you are now.'

Well, the man went home, and immediately he opened the first potion and let a drop fall on to the ball of magic clay, and a soldier looked in at the window, and then emptied a huge sackful of gold into the room. It was more wealth than the poor man had ever imagined was possible, but even so – before he put the stopper back on the potion – he couldn't resist letting just one more drop fall on to the ball of magic clay. The clay quivered in his hand, and then – suddenly – everything in the house turned to gold: the tables, the chairs, the bed, the wardrobe, the cups and plates and knives and forks, the old iron grate, the bucket

by the door, even the door itself – all turned to gold.

Then the man was overcome with greed. 'All the gold in the world can be mine!' he cried, and he poured all the remaining potion on to the ball of magic clay.

Immediately the air was filled with the whirring of thousands of wings, and the sky became black with every conceivable shape and size of bird, all flying towards his house. And each bird carried in its beak a little bag of gold. One by one, they flew over the house, and one by one they dropped their bag of gold, until a huge mountain was formed. Then the birds flew off, and the sky became light again, and the noise of the wings subsided.

The man looked out of his window at the golden mountain outside, and could hardly believe his eyes. 'Now I am, without doubt, the richest man in the world!' he said. Then he built himself a palace and lived like a prince.

It was not long, however, before he heard a banging on his doors, and he went and found a hundred ragged men there. 'Who are you?' he cried.

'Once we were all kings,' they replied, 'but, since you have taken all the gold there is in the world, we have lost our kingdoms, and now we go around on foot, begging for our food.'

'I am sorry to hear that,' said the man, and he gave them each one gold piece, and then turned them out to beg their way again.

Then the man thought to himself: 'What if all those kings should try to steal my gold? I had better get some silver, for then I could pay a hundred soldiers to guard my gold.'

So he took the second potion the wizard had given him, and let a drop fall on to the ball of magic clay and, sure enough, the floors of his palace all turned to silver. Then he let another drop fall, and a silver ball the size of six houses rolled down the road and came to rest in the palace gardens. Then he was overcome with greed to

see what all the silver in the world looked like, and he took the potion and poured it *all* on to the ball of clay. And there was a terrible sound like thunder, and the sky grew black and it started to rain silver pieces. They fell on to roofs and chimney pots and then into the gutters, and formed little streams of silver. And all the streams joined into one great river that flowed down into his palace gardens, and there formed a huge lake of silver.

And he took some of the silver, and hired a hundred soldiers to guard his gold.

But, before long, he heard a banging on his doors, and he went and found a thousand ragged men there. 'Who are *you*?' he cried.

'Once we were all rich merchants,' said the men, 'but, since you have taken all the silver in the world, we have nothing to buy and sell with, and we are ruined as you see.'

'I am sorry for you,' said the man, 'but there is nothing I can do for so many.' And he turned them out of the palace to beg their way in the world.

Then the man said to himself: 'I need to build a chest to hold all that silver and gold. It will be so large that I shall need a lot of wood – I shall need that third potion after all.'

So he took the third potion and poured it all on to the ball of magic clay, and suddenly there was the rushing sound of a million leaves rustling in the wind, and he looked up and there was a forest in the sky coming up from the west. And from the south came another, and from the north and the east as well. And they blotted out the whole sky, and their roots hung down over the earth.

At this all the people looked up and cried: 'What has happened to the day?' And when they found they had no wood to build their homes, no wood to burn on their fires, and no wood for chairs or tables or to make their tools, they all rose up together. And together they beat down the doors of the palace, and took back everything, and the richest man in the world was as poor as he had been before.

Why Birds Sing in the Morning

 LONG, LONG TIME AGO, before you or I were ever thought of, and before there was any distinction between day and night, the King and Queen of the Light had a baby daughter. She was the most beautiful of all creatures. When she first opened her eyes, they were so bright that they filled the world with light. Everywhere she went, creatures were glad to see her. Plants grew at her touch, and animals would come out of their holes just to sit and watch her go by.

In a cave not far away there lived the Witch of the Dark. She too had an only child – a son. He was a sickly boy, he was always pale and sometimes he grew very thin and had to be nursed back to strength.

One day, however, the old Witch of the Dark brought her son to court and proposed a marriage between him and the Princess. When the King of the Light refused, the old Witch flew into a rage, and that very night she and her son broke into the King's palace and stole the beautiful Princess. They took her and locked her up in a dark cave on the other side of the mountains, and there she stayed for a long time. She cried and cried, but it was no good. The Witch would not let the Princess out until she agreed to marry her son.

Meanwhile the animals went to the King and said: 'Where is your daughter? When she is away from us all the world is dark. The plants do not grow and many of us have nothing to eat.'

The King of the Light told the animals what had happened, and the animals all agreed that they would help him look for his daughter.

So the lions and tigers went into the jungle and searched there. The rabbits and moles looked under the earth, and the fish and the turtles searched the seas, but none of them could find any trace of her. Meanwhile the birds were looking in the air and treetops, and the eagle flew off into the mountains. It flew up and up, until it was flying over their very summits. Still it flew on, over the other side and down into a region where it had never been before.

At length, the eagle grew tired and was forced to rest amongst some rocks. He hadn't been there long, however, before he heard a beautiful voice singing a sad song. Immediately he recognized it was the Princess, and he called out to her. But the eagle had only a raucous screech for a voice, and the Princess thought it was the old Witch returning. So she stopped her singing and would not make another sound. The eagle sat there, wondering what to do, when all at once he saw a black speck in the sky. It was the Witch's son, coming to visit the Princess on his mother's broomstick.

The eagle hid, and watched as the Witch's son rolled aside the great stone at the entrance of the cave. Immediately a great brightness flooded out from the cave, as the beautiful Princess came out, and filled everywhere with light. But she had tears in her eyes, and a rainbow shone all around her.

'Ah!' cried the Witch's son. 'I'm tired of waiting!' And he took hold of the beautiful girl, and threw her on the ground. Whereupon the eagle swooped down on them, snapping his beak fiercely at the Witch's son, and lifted the Princess up on his back. The Witch's son grabbed his mother's broomstick, and started hitting out at the eagle. By accident, however, he struck the Princess a blow on the side of her head, so hard that the broomstick broke in two. But the Princess held tight to the eagle, and they soared up into the sky.

The eagle carried the Princess back across the mountains, and wherever they flew they lit up the world that had been lying dark for so long. And the Witch's son got on the broomstick and followed after them. But because the broomstick was broken, he could never quite catch up with them. At length, however, the eagle had to rest again. He let the Princess down off his back and told her to hide, promising to wake her up as soon as the Witch's son had gone past.

So the Princess hid in a cave, and the world went dark once more while the Witch's pale son flew past in the sky. When he had gone, the eagle tried to wake the Princess up, but the blow from the broomstick had made her a bit deaf, and even the eagle with his raucous voice could not wake her. So the eagle asked some sparrows to help him, and they all made as much noise as they could, but still the Princess did not wake up. Eventually the eagle went round all the birds in the neighbourhood and got them all to make as much noise as possible. Finally the Princess awoke, and came out of the cave, lighting the world as she did so.

'Quick!' said the eagle. 'Get on my back – we must be off before the Witch's son

comes past again on his broomstick.' So the Princess got on his back again and away they flew, bringing light to the world wherever they went.

And so they continue to this day, for the Princess and the eagle were turned into the sun, and still they ride high up in the sky; and the Witch's son was turned into the moon. And at the end of every day, when the eagle has to rest, the Princess hides while the Witch's son goes past – and if you look up at the moon, you can still see him with his mother's broken broomstick over his shoulder. The Princess is still as beautiful as ever, now she is the sun, but she is also a little deaf, and that is why all the birds sing as hard as they can every morning in order to wake her up.

The Key

HERE ONCE LIVED A RICH KING whose palace was the largest in the world. On the wall of the palace there hung a huge key that was as long as a man is tall. Now this key was made of pure gold, but it had been made so long ago that no-one could remember what lock it was supposed to open. So the King issued a proclamation that anyone who could discover the lock for which the key had been made should have half his kingdom as a reward.

One day, three brothers came to try their luck.

The eldest one said: 'I am convinced that this is the key to the North Wind.' So the King gave the eldest brother the key, and he rode with it far, far away to the frozen lands, where ice trees grow out of the snow and where even the clouds are hung with icicles. There he found a huge chest lying half-buried in the snow. He tried the key and it fitted the lock but, when he tried to turn it, it was no good. So he loaded the chest on to a cart, and took it back to the King.

Then the second brother said: 'I am sure the key is the key to the South Wind.' So he took the key and rode south to the hot desert, where trees of fire grow out of the burning sands. And there he found a huge door in a mountain. The key fitted the lock perfectly but, when he turned it, it would not work. Just as he was trying it, however, a warm breeze whispered in his ear to look down, and there he found a smaller door which opened when he touched it. So he crept in.

Inside, the mountain was quite hollow right the way across and right the way to the top. The walls were red with the heat, and in the middle was a beautiful

Princess, bound with heavy chains.

'Who are you?' asked the second brother.

But the Princess did not reply. She sat looking straight ahead and would not utter a sound.

The second brother tried the great key on the padlock of her chains, but it would not fit. So he placed the Princess on the back of his horse and took her back to the King.

Then the youngest brother said: 'I think the key is the key to the wind that blows sometimes from West to East and sometimes from East to West.' So he didn't ride anywhere. He took the great key and broke it in two, and from inside it came an oil which they poured on to the lock of the chest. Then the lock opened easily, and inside the chest they found a silver saw, whose teeth were all diamonds, and they took the saw and cut through the chains that bound the Princess, and she turned and cried: 'At last! The spell is broken!' and she told them how a wizard had placed a spell upon her in spite, because she would not be his wife, and how she could only be rescued by someone she would love but could not marry.

Then the second brother leapt up and cried: 'I rescued you from the hollow mountain of the South Wind!'

Then the eldest brother leapt up and said: 'But it was the silver saw that freed you from the spell, and *I* brought that back from the frozen lands!'

Finally the youngest brother stood up and said: 'But it was *I* who broke the golden key and, if I had not done that, the chest would not have opened and your chains would never have been cut.'

The Princess looked at all three of them and said: 'The wizard's curse has indeed come true. All three of you have rescued me, and I love you all equally, and it is certain I cannot marry all three of you.'

So the youngest brother took one half of the golden key as his reward, and the second brother took the other half, and the eldest brother took the silver saw with the diamond teeth. And all three were then wealthier than anyone else in the kingdom. But they were never truly happy, for they continued to love the beautiful Princess, and she continued to love all three of them equally, and they could never marry.

And many times they all four sighed together and sometimes they even wished they had left the golden key hanging on the palace wall.

The Wine of Li-Po

N THE LAND OF LI-PO THEY MADE a very special wine. It was deep red in colour, it tasted like nectar, and it kept for ever. But it had one other quality which made it more special than any other wine in the world – whoever drank the wine of Li-Po would speak the truth and only the truth as long as its influence lasted.

Now you might think that a wine with such wonderful properties would be in great demand, and that the vineyards of Li-Po would have had difficulty in producing enough grapes. But quite the reverse was true. It seemed that fewer and fewer people dared to drink the wine of Li-Po for fear that they would have to tell the truth, and the cellars became filled with barrels and bottles of the wine that no-one would buy.

At length there was only one wine-maker left in the whole of Li-Po. 'I cannot understand,' he said, 'why everyone is so afraid of the truth. In my father's time, everyone drank the wine and enjoyed it. And if they had to tell the truth for half a day after, it was no matter to them.'

One day, however, the King of a distant country got to hear of the famous wine of Li-Po. So he said to his Lord Chancellor: 'Lord Chancellor, it is time I found out who are my trusty subjects and who are not. I want you to arrange for everyone in my kingdom to drink the wine of Li-Po, and to present themselves to me for questioning.'

When the Lord Chancellor heard this command, he shook with fear, for he had many dark secrets that he dreaded the King might find out. But he smiled and said: 'An excellent idea, Your Majesty. May I be the first to try it out?'

'Good!' said the King. 'See to it straight away.'

So the Lord Chancellor ordered all the barrels of wine in Li-Po to be bought up, and carried in carts over the country to his own land. There the wine was put into bottles, and on every bottle was written somebody's name. Then the bottles were carefully placed in a huge rack in the main market-place, and seven soldiers were put on duty to guard them day and night.

The Lord Chancellor, meanwhile, was racking his brains to think how he could avoid the test himself, for fear that he should reveal any of his own dark and guilty secrets to the King. So too were all the other members of the King's Council, for they *all* had dark and guilty secrets. The same went for all the other lords and ladies and lawyers and doctors and innkeepers and shopkeepers. In fact, every single person in the land was trying his hardest to think how he could avoid drinking the wine of Li-Po and having to tell the truth to the King.

Then the Lord Chancellor hit upon a plan. He had a sleeping potion put into the guards' drink, and then, at dead of night when they had all fallen fast asleep, the Chancellor crept down to the market square, and took the bottle of wine which bore his name, emptied it out, and refilled it with ordinary wine. Then he made his way home, satisfied that when his turn came he would not have to tell the truth.

The same plan had also occurred to the other members of the King's Council, and each one of them crept down to the market square during the nights that followed, and each, unknown to the others, substituted ordinary wine in the bottle which bore his name. It was not long, of course, before word got out that the guards were asleep all night, and very soon all the other lords and ladies had taken the opportunity to do the self-same thing. So too did all the lawyers and doctors and innkeepers and shopkeepers and craftsmen. In short, by the time the day of the tasting came, every one of those bottles of the wine of Li-Po had been emptied and refilled with ordinary wine.

The whole town was buzzing with excitement. The streets were full and the market-place was bursting with the crowds. Everyone in the kingdom was there – except for one notorious robber, who had been hiding up in the hills for several years.

As soon as it was light, the King took his place on his throne, and summoned the Lord Chancellor forward.

'My Lord Chancellor,' he said, 'since you are the most eminent of all my subjects, you shall commence.'

The Lord Chancellor smiled, filled his goblet and drank it down, and said: 'Now I am ready to answer any questions you wish, Your Majesty.'

'Very well,' said the King, 'first tell me: are you a good and loyal subject?'

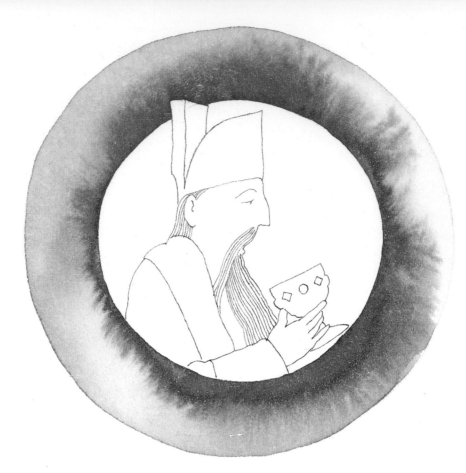

'Indeed I am!' replied the Lord Chancellor, although at that very moment he was plotting to overthrow the King.

'Secondly', said the King, 'do you think I'm a wise ruler?'

'Indeed I *do*!' exclaimed the Lord Chancellor, although secretly he thought: 'What a fool the king is making of himself!'

'And lastly,' said the King, 'how does the wine of Li-Po taste?'

'It tastes like nectar distilled from all the flowers of heaven!' said the Lord Chancellor.

'Very good,' said the King. 'You may step down.'

The next to drink the wine was the Prime Minister, and the King asked him the same three questions, and the Prime Minister made similar answers – although he was really no better than the Lord Chancellor.

And so they went on through all the King's Council, and all the lords and ladies, and the lawyers and doctors and the townsfolk and all the countryfolk. And, because they had all emptied the wine of Li-Po out of the bottles that bore their names and replaced it with ordinary wine, none of them was afraid of answering any of the King's questions.

Well, the questioning went on all that day and all the next day, and all the day after that, until – just as they were questioning the very last subject of all – some soldiers arrived with the robber, whom they had caught stealing in broad daylight, while everyone was in the city. They hauled him up before the King, and the King ordered him to drink the wine of Li-Po, and then answer the questions that he

would put to him.

Now the robber did not know that all the wine of Li-Po had been poured away, and so he took the cup with fear and trembling. But he drank it all the same. Then he faced the King.

'Firstly, are you a good and loyal subject?' asked the King.

'You know me for what I am,' replied the robber. 'I've robbed your kingdom for many years.'

'Shame!' cried all the people.

'Secondly, do you think I'm a wise ruler?' asked the King.

'I've nothing to lose by telling the truth,' replied the robber, 'and the truth is: a wise ruler would decide for himself which of his subjects he could trust.'

'Traitor!' shouted the crowd.

'Lastly,' said the King, 'how does the wine of Li-Po taste?'

'I'm sure I don't know,' replied the robber. 'I've never tasted it, and this is just ordinary wine.'

At which words a silence fell over the market-place, and everyone stared at the ground. And the King rose and said: 'Is this the only person in my kingdom who dares to tell the truth?'

There and then he dismissed the Lord Chancellor, and appointed the robber in his place, saying: 'I would rather be served by a thief than a hypocrite.' And from that day forth, the wine of Li-Po was never seen in his kingdom again, for it had served its purpose – even though not one drop of it had been drunk.

The Island of Purple Fruits

SAILOR WAS ONCE SHIPWRECKED on a strange island. He swam ashore and then turned and watched his ship sink beneath the waves. But he did not despair.

'I will build myself another boat to take me home,' he said. 'And I will also build a great fire that I will light to attract the attention of any ship that passes.' So he got to work, and in the meantime he lived off the fruits and berries that grew there in abundance.

On this island, however, there was one kind of fruit that he could never taste. It was large and purple, and it grew high up on the tallest of all the trees. The trunk of the tree was perfectly smooth and impossible to climb but, as he gazed up at those purple fruits, the sailor said to himself: 'I am sure that those are the most delicious fruits on the island. I am going to taste them, no matter what.'

So he stopped building his boat, and built himself a ladder instead, which he leant up against the tree. Then he climbed to the top, picked a fruit, and ate it. It tasted more delicious than anything else he had ever eaten in his life, and that night he dreamt a wonderful dream. He dreamt he had finished his boat, and that it was a fine vessel with tall sails. On it he sailed back in his dream across the vast ocean to his wife and children, and he was truly happy at last.

When he woke up, he took another bite of the purple fruit, and fell asleep again, and this time he dreamt that he built himself a suit of feathers, and in this suit he flew like a bird over the waters and over his own home, and his wife and children came out and waved up at him, and he flew to the King's palace, and the King gave

him jewels and gold and a fine house, where he lived with his family, and they were all truly happy.

When he woke up, it was broad daylight, and there in the bay was a great ship.

'At last!' he cried. 'I'm saved!' And he ran down to the shore and waved, but the ship was already well out to sea, and no-one saw him. So he ran to his fire, but it had gone out and, before he could light it, the ship was but a speck on the horizon.

The poor shipwrecked sailor sat down with his head in his hands in despair. Then he took another bite of the purple fruit, and once more he slept and dreamt that he was truly happy.

Many months passed, and the sailor began to eat nothing but the purple fruit, and he dreamt all the night and most of the day – beautiful dreams in which he was truly happy, and so were his wife and children. Little by little, he forgot about building his boat that was going to take him home, and, whenever the occasional ship passed the island, he never even noticed it, and the fire remained unlit. Thus, although the sailor returned home time and time again in his dreams, the years passed and still he remained on that desert island.

One day, however, a tall ship entered the bay and sent a search party ashore to gather fresh water and fruit. There they came across the ragged figure of the sailor, sleeping happily under a purple fruit tree. They could not wake him, however hard they tried, and so they picked him up and carried him down to the ship. There they placed him in a bed and put to sea once more.

When the sailor eventually awoke and learnt what had happened, his rescuers expected him to leap for joy, but instead he cried out: 'Oh! Now I shall never be truly happy again, for I shall never be able to eat any more of that purple fruit!'

There was no going back, however, and eventually they returned him to his own country. There he made his way home at long last. When he got there, he found it had all changed from his dreams, for he had been away so long that his children had grown up, and the pretty young wife that he had left behind had grown old with work and care.

Nevertheless, he took her in his arms, and said: 'Why! I am as happy now as I was in my dreams on the island of purple fruits!'

But his wife said: 'How can you compare the happiness of a dream with true happiness?'

'But it *was* true happiness,' replied the sailor. 'No-one could be happier than I was in those dreams.'

But his wife looked at him and said: 'In your dreams on the island of purple fruits, did you dream that we were happy too?'

'Indeed I did!' said the sailor. 'And that made my happiness complete.'

'Yet it was just a dream,' said his wife, 'for we were still sad, believing you were dead. But now you have returned to us, you know it's not a dream, and that knowledge – surely – *is* true happiness.'

The sailor kissed his wife and children and after that, although he often thought of the island of purple fruits and the happiness of dreams, he never spoke of either again.

The Beast with a Thousand Teeth

A LONG TIME AGO, in a land far away, the most terrible beast that ever lived roamed the countryside. It had four eyes, six legs and a thousand teeth. In the morning it would gobble up men as they went to work in the fields. In the afternoon it would break into lonely farms and eat up mothers and children as they sat down to lunch, and at night it would stalk the streets of the towns, looking for its supper.

In the biggest of all the towns, there lived a pastrycook and his wife, and they had a small son whose name was Sam. One morning, as Sam was helping his father to make pastries, he heard that the Mayor had offered a reward of ten bags of gold to anyone who could rid the city of the beast.

'Oh,' said Sam, 'wouldn't I just like to win those ten bags of gold!'

'Nonsense!' said his father. 'Put those pastries in the oven.'

That afternoon, they heard that the King himself had offered a reward of a hundred bags of gold to anyone who could rid the kingdom of the beast.

'Oooh! Wouldn't I just like to win those hundred bags of gold,' said Sam.

'You're too small,' said his father. 'Now run along and take those cakes to the Palace before it gets dark.'

So Sam set off for the Palace with a tray of cakes balanced on his head. But he was so busy thinking of the hundred bags of gold that he lost his way, and soon it began to grow dark.

'Oh dear!' said Sam. 'The beast will be coming soon to look for his supper. I'd better hurry home.'

So he turned and started to hurry home as fast as he could. But he was utterly and completely lost, and he didn't know which way to turn. Soon it grew very dark. The streets were deserted, and everyone was safe inside, and had bolted and barred their doors for fear of the beast.

Poor Sam ran up this street and down the next, but he couldn't find the way home. Then suddenly – in the distance – he heard a sound like thunder, and he knew that the beast with a thousand teeth was approaching the city!

Sam ran up to the nearest house, and started to bang on the door.

'Let me in!' he cried. 'I'm out in the streets, and the beast is approaching the city! Listen!' And he could hear the sound of the beast getting nearer and nearer. The ground shook and the windows rattled in their frames. But the people inside said no – if they opened the door, the beast might get in and eat them too.

So poor Sam ran up to the next house, and banged as hard as he could on their door, but the people told him to go away.

Then he heard a roar, and he heard the beast coming down the street, and he ran as hard as he could. But no matter how hard he ran, he could hear the beast getting nearer . . . and nearer. . . . And he glanced over his shoulder – and there it was at the end of the street! Poor Sam in his fright dropped his tray, and hid under some steps. And the beast got nearer and nearer until it was right on top of him, and it bent down and its terrible jaws went SNACK! and it gobbled up the tray of cakes, and then it turned on Sam.

Sam plucked up all his courage and shouted as loud as he could: 'Don't eat me, Beast! Wouldn't you rather have some more cakes?'

The beast stopped and looked at Sam, and then it looked back at the empty tray, and it said: 'Well . . . they *were* very nice cakes . . . I liked the pink ones particularly. But there are no more left, so I'll just have to eat you. . . .' And it reached under the steps where poor Sam was hiding, and pulled him out in its great horny claws.

'Oh . . . p-p-please!' cried Sam. 'If you don't eat me, I'll make you some more. I'll make you lots of good things, for I'm the son of the best pastrycook in the land.'

'Will you make more of those pink ones?' asked the beast.

'Oh yes! I'll make you as many pink ones as you can eat!' cried Sam.

'Very well,' said the beast, and put poor Sam in his pocket, and carried him home to his lair.

The beast lived in a dark and dismal cave. The floor was littered with the bones of the people it had eaten, and the stone walls were marked with lines, where the beast used to sharpen its teeth. But Sam got to work right away, and started to bake as many cakes as he could for the beast. And when he ran out of flour or eggs or anything else, the beast would run back into town to get them, although it never paid for anything.

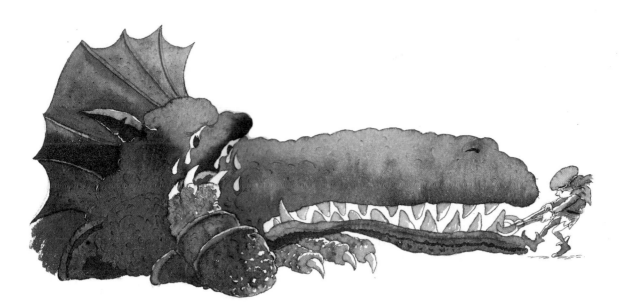

Sam cooked and baked, and he made scones and éclairs and meringues and sponge cakes and shortbread and doughnuts. But the beast looked at them and said, 'You haven't made any pink ones!'

'Just a minute!' said Sam, and he took all the cakes and he covered every one of them in pink icing.

'There you are,' said Sam, 'they're *all* pink ones!'

'Great!' said the beast and ate the lot.

Well, the beast grew so fond of Sam's cakes that it shortly gave up eating people altogether, and it stayed at home in its cave eating and eating, and growing fatter and fatter. This went on for a whole year, until one morning Sam woke up to find the beast rolling around groaning and beating the floor of the cave. Of course you can guess what was the matter with it.

'Oh dear,' said Sam, 'I'm afraid it's all that pink icing that has given you toothache.'

Well, the toothache got worse and worse and, because the beast had a thousand teeth, it was soon suffering from the worst toothache that anyone in the whole history of the world has ever suffered from. It lay on its side and held its head and roared in agony, until Sam began to feel quite sorry for it. The beast howled and howled with pain, until it could stand it no longer. 'Please, Sam, help me!' it cried.

'Very well,' said Sam. 'Sit still and open your mouth.'

So the beast sat very still and opened its mouth, while Sam got a pair of pliers and took out every single tooth in that beast's head.

Well, when the beast had lost all its thousand teeth, it couldn't eat people any more. So Sam took it home and went to the Mayor and claimed ten bags of gold as his reward. Then he went to the King and claimed the hundred bags of gold as his reward. Then he went back and lived with his father and mother once more, and the beast helped in the pastryshop, and took cakes to the Palace every day, and everyone forgot they had ever been afraid of the beast with a thousand teeth.

Far-Away Castle

A TRAVELLER ONCE STOPPED TO ASK an old woman the name of a castle that stood on a hill close by.

'Well, nobody rightly knows its name,' said the old woman, 'but round here they do call it Far-Away Castle.'

'That's an odd name,' said the traveller, 'for it doesn't look so very far from here.'

'Ah no,' said the woman, 'it don't look very far, do it?'

'It couldn't take me more than an hour to walk there, could it?' said the traveller.

'I wouldn't know,' said the old woman.

'But you must know how far away it is.'

'Can't say as I do,' said the old woman.

'Well, that's where I'm going,' said the traveller, and he set off, shaking his head at the ignorance of country folk.

Well, he walked for an hour, and he walked for two hours, and he walked for three hours – up hill and down hill. And when he looked up the castle, it seemed not an inch closer.

'Bless my soul!' said the traveller. 'I must be walking round it in circles, for I'm certainly not getting any nearer!' So he left the road, and headed off across the fields straight for the castle.

Well, he'd been walking for another hour or so when he found himself entering a dark and gloomy forest. He got a firm grip on his staff, and took out his great knife, in case he met with any bears or wolves. Then on he went through the forest.

At first he followed a path, but it soon petered out, and the forest grew thicker and the undergrowth grew denser until he was forced to cut his way through with his knife. At length, however, the forest began to thin out again and he began to see the light shining through the trees once more, and he knew he was getting to the other side. But when he finally stepped out from the forest and looked up, he couldn't believe his eyes: there was the castle on the hill above him, but not one inch closer than it had been before.

The traveller redoubled his efforts, and walked as fast as he could until night fell, and he was still no nearer his goal. Wearily he wrapped himself up in his cloak and lay down to sleep.

Hardly had he shut his eyes, when he heard a voice say: 'You'd better give up, you know.'

He turned round, and found the old woman sitting up in a tree.

'I shan't give up!' cried the traveller. 'I'll reach that castle tomorrow – you'll see!'

'I suppose I shall,' said the old woman, 'but remember what I told you.' And with that she folded up like black paper, into a bat that flew out of the branches and away into the night.

The traveller lay down to sleep again, and he dreamt he could hear elfin music, borne faintly upon the breeze, all the time he slept.

The next day, he woke up, and there, sure enough, was the castle sitting above him on the hill – not very far away at all.

'I can reach that by lunchtime!' he cried, and he seized his staff, put his pack on his back, and walked as hard and as fast as he could. And all the time, he never once took his eyes off that castle.

But lunchtime came, and still he was no nearer. No matter what path he took or how fast he went, it made not a scrap of difference. By supper-time, he was still no nearer the castle.

He sat down with his head between his hands, and heaved a big sigh.

'That castle's enchanted, ' he said to himself. 'The old woman was right – I might as well give up trying.' And he got to his feet and walked round the corner, and there – to his amazement – was the castle, and the little old woman was sitting outside it.

'Ah!' she cried. 'So you gave up trying at last, did you? It's the only way to get here, though no-one ever believes it.'

And with that she opened the door of the castle, and the traveller went in.

Dr Bonocolus's Devil

R BONOCOLUS WAS A VERY CLEVER MAN. He lived a long time ago in a distant land. He was very proud of his learning, and he enjoyed performing in public debates, where he could show how much cleverer he was than anyone else.

One day, however, Dr Bonocolus decided to sell his soul to the Devil. He read in a big book a certain number of magic spells, and late that night, he lit a candle in his study, drew some lines on the floor and summoned the Devil to appear before him. There was a flash and a puff of smoke and the smell of brimstone and, for just a moment, he thought he could hear the roaring of hell-fire. But before he could change his mind, there in front of him stood a short gentleman in grey with a pen tucked behind his ear.

'You're not the Devil!' cried Dr Bonocolus.

'Er . . . no,' replied the figure in grey. 'The Devil is extremely busy at this moment in time. I'm his official representative. Now, if you'd just like to give me your details, we can get on with the sale.' And he opened a large leather book that he was carrying.

'Wait a moment!' said Dr Bonocolus. 'I wanted to see the Devil himself! I don't want to sell my soul to some half-witted underling!'

'The Devil *does* apologize, most sincerely,' said the gentleman in grey, 'but it's just a question of feasibility. If you don't want to do the deal with me, that's quite understandable – but we'll just have to let the sale go. We have more than enough to choose from as it is. It's a buyer's market at the moment, you know.'

In the end, Dr Bonocolus agreed to sell his soul to the Devil's representative on what seemed very favourable terms. For thirty years, the Devil would give Dr Bonocolus unlimited wealth, fame and magical powers. At the end of thirty years, Dr Bonocolus would have to sit and play backgammon with the Devil for ever.

Dr Bonocolus made a cut on his arm, and was just about to sign in his own blood when the Devil's representative stopped him. He looked around rather furtively and then lowered his voice and said: 'Look . . . officially, I shouldn't be telling you this, but . . . well, are you quite sure you know what you're doing?'

'Of course I am!' said Dr Bonocolus. 'You forget I'm the cleverest man in the world! I've thought out exactly what I will do with my thirty years, and after that the Devil can torture me as much as he likes. I've worked it out as a mathematical equation and the worst pain he could inflict on me will not outweigh the amount of pleasure I will be able to cram into thirty years!'

'He may *not* torture you,' said the Devil's representative.

'Then so much the better!' said Dr Bonocolus.

'It may be much worse than torture.'

'Impossible!' cried Dr Bonocolus. 'I've thought about every conceivable thing he could do to me, and I'm prepared for anything.'

The Devil's representative glanced over his shoulder and lowered his voice even more. 'Look,' he said, 'I know you're the cleverest man in the world right now but, no matter what you've imagined, I can tell you it will be worse.'

'I can't believe it!' said Dr Bonocolus, and he dipped his pen into the blood from his arm, and signed his name in the big book and on two contracts. Then the Devil's representative went away, and for thirty years Dr Bonocolus became not only the cleverest man in the world, but also the richest and the most respected and the most admired. Naturally he told no-one about his deal with the Devil, and everywhere he was revered for the brilliance of his mind, the sharpness of his wit, and the depth of his understanding. He learnt every language in the world, and there was no branch of science or art at which he did not become a master.

Finally, though, his thirty years were up, and he had to go down to Hell to face the Devil, who was now his master. He had prepared himself well for his ordeal, however. He had studied every existing portrait of the Devil, and had steeped himself in every picture of evil, ugliness and horror in order that he would not be aghast at the Devil's appearance.

As he was taken down into Hell by numerous nasty little creatures who pulled his hair and tugged his clothes, he felt quite cheerful and confident that he could cope with the worst that the Devil could do. To tell the truth, he felt quite proud of himself, for he had been master of the world while he lived, and now he was prepared to submit to one who was greater than himself. Indeed, he flattered himself that the Devil might well appreciate his fine wit and intelligence, and even

find some use for his talents.

At length, Dr Bonocolus was brought to the Devil's audience chamber. The Devil's throne was standing there empty, surrounded by a host of ugly creatures so evil in their appearance that even Dr Bonocolus began to feel uneasy.

Then a scaly monster, whose smell was so loathsome that it made the Doctor feel sick, slouched towards the throne, and put out a grasping hand towards the Doctor, so that he suddenly trembled and was gripped by a fear of something unimaginable. And an unearthly voice croaked: 'Dr Bonocolus . . . prepare to meet the Devil himself!'

Even Dr Bonocolus felt a little weak at the knees and a little apprehensive, remembering what the Devil's representative had said to him all those years ago: 'No matter what you've imagined . . . it will be worse.'

Suddenly there was a flash, and the throne was engulfed in smoke. Dr Bonocolus braced himself and then there he was – face to face with the Devil . . . his new master. Dr Bonocolus's jaw dropped, and he went cold with horror. The Devil's representative had been right, of course . . . but it wasn't the hideousness of the Devil's features, nor even the cold brutality of that face that was worse than any torture to Dr Bonocolus. It was the appalling realization, as he gazed into the Devil's eyes, that the Devil was clearly stupid.

'Of course!' cried Dr Bonocolus. 'It's so obvious!' But it was too late. The cleverest man in the world had sold his soul to a fool.

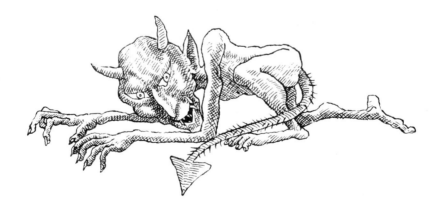

The Boat That Went Nowhere

NCE UPON A TIME A POOR WIDOW HAD A SON called Tom, whom she loved very much. But she was so poor that there was often not enough food in the house, and young Tom was often hungry.

One day in the middle of winter, when the pond was frozen over and icicles hung from the hedges, Tom's mother went to the larder and said: 'There is nothing at all to eat. Whatever shall we do?' and she sat down and wept.

'Don't cry, Mother,' said Tom, 'I'll go and seek my fortune and bring back enough money so you will never have to worry again.' And he tied his only pair of boots up in a handkerchief and set off to seek his fortune.

He hadn't gone very far before he came to a great house with huge gates and beautiful gardens and fountains. 'There must be a lot of money here,' thought Tom to himself. 'I'm sure I'll be able to earn enough in this place so that my mother will never go short again.' So he walked boldly up to the great house and knocked at the door.

A little old man in black answered the door and said: 'What do you want?' When Tom told him, the little old man looked very angry and said: 'There's no money for you here!' and set a dog on poor Tom that chased him off.

Well, he travelled on until at length he came to a city, where a rich merchant lived. He knocked on the door of the rich merchant's house, and a fat man in a wig asked: 'What do you want?'

'I want to earn some money so that my mother will not go hungry again.'

'Very well, you can work here,' said the fat man, and led Tom out into the garden at the back of the house.

'All you have to do', he said, 'is to climb into the sack that hangs from that tree over there and stay in it for a year and a day.'

'What's the point of that?' asked Tom.

'Never you mind,' said the fat man in the wig. 'I'll pay you more money than you've ever had in your life and feed you well into the bargain.'

'Very well,' said Tom and climbed into the sack. But just as night fell, and Tom was growing very bored and wondering how on earth he was going to last out a whole year in that sack, an owl settled on the branch above him and cried: 'Towit-to-woo, towit-to-woo.' But it seemed to Tom that it was saying: 'You'll sit life through! You'll sit life through!'

'He's right!' cried Tom. 'I won't make my mother happy by wasting my life in this sack! I'll find some better way of getting rich.' And he jumped down from the sack and walked out of the garden into the night.

It was very cold and dark and a little frightening, but he thought to himself: 'I must keep going.' Eventually he saw a fire glowing in the distance. 'Ah, I shall at least be able to warm myself there,' he said.

When he reached the fire, he found it was a roaring furnace, and there was a huge man, stripped to the waist and sweating as he shovelled coal into the furnace as hard as he could.

'May I warm myself by your fire?' asked Tom. The man didn't answer, but he kept on shovelling the coal.

'What are you doing?' asked Tom.

The man paused for a moment and looked at Tom and said: 'I'm earning more money than you've ever set eyes on!'

'May I help you?' asked Tom.

'You can take over just as soon as I finish,' said the man.

'When will that be?' asked Tom.

'Oh, not long,' said the man. 'I just have to finish feeding the fire, and then climb to the top of the chimney, and I'm done.' So Tom sat down on the grass to wait his turn, and by and by he fell fast asleep.

When he woke up it was broad daylight, and the huge man was still busy shovelling away as hard as ever.

'When do you finish feeding the fire?' asked Tom.

'When it's had enough,' replied the man without stopping.

'But a fire can never have enough!' said Tom, and just then he noticed that the furnace was at the bottom of a chimney that had steps running round and round all the way up the outside. And Tom looked up and up, and he saw that the chimney went straight up into the sky – for ever – as if it had no top.

'I'm afraid I can't wait for you to finish,' said Tom, and he picked up his pack and set off again. And he walked down to the harbour, where the great ships lay at

anchor, and he asked to be taken on. But everywhere they told him he was too young and too small to be of any use on a great ship.

At length, however, he came to a queer little boat, smaller than the rest and painted red and white. The captain was leaning over the side, and so Tom said: 'Could you use another hand?'

'Aye,' said the captain.

'Where are you going?' asked Tom.

'Nowhere,' said the captain.

'Well, I'll get nowhere if I stay here, so I might as well go with you,' said Tom and he climbed aboard.

Straight away the captain ordered the sails to be set and the anchor weighed and that little boat set off on the high seas. And the winds blew it along until it was out of sight of land, and they sailed into the setting sun. How many days and how many nights they sailed for, I don't know, but one morning there was a shout: 'Land ahoy!'

And they all looked over the side of the boat and there, sure enough, was a beautiful country with tall mountains. And as they got closer they saw that the mountains were shining white with red tops. And as they got closer still, they saw that they weren't mountains at all, but huge cities reaching up to the clouds.

'Where are we?' cried Tom.

'Nowhere,' said the captain, and they all got out.

Tom couldn't believe his eyes. On each side of them were flowerbeds full of flowers, and each one of their petals was a pound note. In front of them stretched a lawn down to a river of pure silver. When he looked at the trees they were made out of solid gold and the leaves were emeralds, and everywhere piles of precious jewels lay around for the taking. 'We're rich!' he cried.

'You haven't seen anything yet,' smiled the captain, and they all set off for the great city that glittered and shone before them. As they walked, birds flew above them, dropping pearls and rubies into their upturned hats, and wild deer ran up to them and laid golden sticks at their feet.

Eventually they reached the gates of the shining city, and the captain pulled on a golden chain.

A peal of bells rang out in welcome and a boy opened the door wide and said: 'We are glad to see you in the Forgotten City, come in,' and took them into a pure white square, where the sound of laughter echoed all around. And before Tom could blink, a table had been set out for them with all the food they could eat and all the wine they could drink. And the townspeople brought them presents and played them music, and gave up their own beds so that the travellers should sleep well.

And there they stayed for many weeks, until at length Tom said: 'I must go back to my mother.'

The captain said: 'Very well! Take the boat.'

'But what about you and the others?' asked Tom

'That's all right,' said the captain, 'we can easily get another.' So Tom loaded up the boat with all the gold and silver and jewels he could carry and set off back across the ocean.

Well, he hadn't sailed very far before he was caught in a terrible dark storm. The waters raged and the little boat was tossed here and there until at length it took on so much water that it sank to the bottom of the sea. And Tom went down too, until a dolphin came up and put him on its back and swam with him until they got to the very river that ran past his own home.

Tom was still as poor as ever but, when he saw his mother, he smiled and said: 'Well, I have discovered that nobody with money will part with it, unless I waste my life away, and that those whose *only* desire is wealth will never rest content, and that the only place where there is enough for all and everyone is kind and generous is Nowhere. So, Mother, what shall I do?'

And his mother said: 'Sit by the fire, and I shall make soup from your stories, and we'll have our hopes for bread.'

And that is what they did.